FANTASY ON PARADE

WALT DISNEY
FANTASY
ON PARADE

WITH ILLUSTRATIONS BY THE WALT DISNEY STUDIO

THE WALT DISNEY PARADE
OF FUN, FACT, FANTASY AND FICTION

GOLDEN PRESS · NEW YORK

Western Publishing Company, Inc.
Racine, Wisconsin

Revised Edition

Copyright © 1977 by Walt Disney Productions. Stories and pictures in this book previously copyrighted © 1974, 1972, 1970, 1969, 1968, 1965, 1953, 1951, 1944, 1941 by Walt Disney Productions.

CONTENTS

Winnie-the-Pooh
and Eeyore's Birthday

Eeyore, the old grey Donkey, stood by the side of the stream, and looked at himself in the water.

"Pathetic," he said. "That's what it is. Pathetic."

He turned and walked slowly down the stream for twenty yards, splashed across it, and walked slowly back on the other side. Then he looked at himself in the water again.

"As I thought," he said. "No better from *this* side. But nobody minds. Nobody cares. Pathetic, that's what it is."

There was a crackling noise in the bracken behind him, and out came Pooh.

"Good morning, Eeyore," said Pooh.

"Good morning, Pooh Bear," said Eeyore gloomily. "If it *is* a good morning," he said. "Which I doubt," said he.

"Why, what's the matter?"

"Nothing, Pooh Bear, nothing. We can't all, and some of us don't. That's all there is to it."

"Can't all *what*?" said Pooh, rubbing his nose.

"Gaiety. Song-and-dance. Here we go round the mulberry bush."

"Oh!" said Pooh. He thought for a long time, and then asked, "What mulberry bush is that?"

"Bon-hommy," went on Eeyore gloomily.

"French word meaning bonhommy," he explained. "I'm not complaining, but There It Is."

Pooh sat down on a large stone, and tried to think this out. It sounded to him like a riddle, and he was never much good at riddles, being a Bear of Very Little Brain. So he sang *Cottleston Pie* instead:

> Cottleston, Cottleston, Cottleston Pie,
> A fly can't bird, but a bird can fly.
> Ask me a riddle and I reply:
> *"Cottleston, Cottleston, Cottleston Pie."*

That was the first verse. When he had finished it, Eeyore didn't actually say that he didn't like it, so Pooh very kindly sang the second verse to him:

> Cottleston, Cottleston, Cottleston Pie,
> A fish can't whistle and neither can I.
> Ask me a riddle and I reply:
> *"Cottleston, Cottleston, Cottleston Pie."*

Eeyore still said nothing at all, so Pooh hummed the third verse quietly to himself:

> Cottleston, Cottleston, Cottleston Pie,
> Why does a chicken, I don't know why.

> Ask me a riddle and I reply:
> *"Cottleston, Cottleston, Cottleston Pie."*

"That's right," said Eeyore. "Sing. Umty-tiddly, umty-too. Here we go gathering Nuts and May. Enjoy yourself."

"I am," said Pooh.

"Some can," said Eeyore.

"Why, what's the matter?"

"*Is* anything the matter?"

"You seem so sad, Eeyore."

"Sad? Why should I be sad? It's my birthday. The happiest day of the year."

"Your birthday?" said Pooh in great surprise.

"Of course it is. Can't you see? Look at all the presents I have had." He waved a foot from side to side. "Look at the birthday cake. Candles and pink sugar."

Pooh looked—first to the right and then to the left.

"Presents?" said Pooh. "Birthday cake?" said Pooh. "*Where?*"

"Can't you see them?"

"No," said Pooh.

"Neither can I," said Eeyore. "Joke," he explained. "Ha ha!"

Pooh scratched his head, being a little puzzled by all this.

"But is it really your birthday?" he asked.

"It is."

7

"Oh! Well, Many happy returns of the day, Eeyore."

"And many happy returns to you, Pooh Bear."

"But it isn't *my* birthday."

"No, it's mine."

"But you said 'Many happy returns'————"

"Well, why not? You don't always want to be miserable on my birthday, do you?"

"Oh, I see," said Pooh.

"It's bad enough," said Eeyore, almost breaking down, "being miserable myself, what with no presents and no cake and no candles, and no proper notice taken of me at all, but if everybody else is going to be miserable too————"

This was too much for Pooh. "Stay there!" he called to Eeyore, as he turned and hurried back home as quick as he could; for he felt that he must get poor Eeyore a present of *some* sort at once, and he could always think of a proper one afterwards.

Outside his house he found Piglet, jumping up and down trying to reach the knocker.

"Hallo, Piglet," he said.

"Hallo, Pooh," said Piglet.

"What are *you* trying to do?"

"I was trying to reach the knocker," said Piglet. "I just came round————"

"Let me do it for you," said Pooh kindly. So he reached up and knocked at the door. "I have just seen Eeyore," he began, "and poor Eeyore is in a Very Sad Condition, because it's his birthday, and nobody has taken any notice of it, and he's very Gloomy —you know what Eeyore is—and there he was, and————What a long time whoever lives here is answering this door." And he knocked again.

"But Pooh," said Piglet, "it's your own house!"

"Oh!" said Pooh. "So it is," he said. "Well, let's go in."

So in they went. The first thing Pooh did

was to go to the cupboard to see if he had quite a small jar of honey left; and he had, so he took it down.

"I'm giving this to Eeyore," he explained, "as a present. What are *you* going to give?"

"Couldn't I give it too?" said Piglet. "From both of us?"

"No," said Pooh. "That would *not* be a good plan."

"All right, then, I'll give him a balloon. I've got one left from my party. I'll go and get it now, shall I?"

"That, Piglet, is a *very* good idea. It is just what Eeyore wants to cheer him up. Nobody can be uncheered with a balloon."

So off Piglet trotted; and in the other direction went Pooh, with his jar of honey.

It was a warm day, and he had a long way to go. He hadn't gone more than half-way when a sort of funny feeling began to

creep all over him. It began at the tip of his nose and trickled all through him and out at the soles of his feet. It was just as if somebody inside him were saying, "Now then, Pooh, time for a little something."

"Dear, dear," said Pooh, "I didn't know it was as late as that." So he sat down and took the top off his jar of honey. "Lucky I brought this with me," he thought. "Many a bear going out on a warm day like this would never have thought of bringing a little something with him." And he began to eat.

"Now let me see," he thought, as he took his last lick of the inside of the jar, "where was I going? Ah, yes, Eeyore." He got up slowly.

And then, suddenly, he remembered. He had eaten Eeyore's birthday present!

"*Bother!*" said Pooh. "What *shall* I do? I *must* give him *something*."

For a little while he couldn't think of anything. Then he thought: "Well, it's a very nice pot, even if there's no honey in it, and if I washed it clean, and got somebody to write '*A Happy Birthday*' on it, Eeyore could keep things in it, which might be Useful." So, as he was just passing the Hundred Acre Wood, he went inside to call on Owl, who lived there.

"Good morning, Owl," he said.

"Good morning, Pooh," said Owl.

"Many happy returns of Eeyore's birthday," said Pooh.

"Oh, is that what it is?"

"What are you giving him, Owl?"

"What are *you* giving him, Pooh?"

"I'm giving him a Useful Pot to Keep Things In, and I wanted to ask you————"

"Is this it?" said Owl, taking it out of Pooh's paw.

"Yes, and I wanted to ask you————"

"Somebody has been keeping honey in it," said Owl.

"You can keep *anything* in it," said Pooh earnestly. "It's Very Useful like that. And I wanted to ask you————"

"You ought to write '*A Happy Birthday*' on it."

"*That* was what I wanted to ask you," said Pooh. "Because my spelling is Wobbly. It's good spelling but it Wobbles, and the letters get in the wrong places. Would *you* write 'A Happy Birthday' on it for me?"

"It's a nice pot," said Owl, looking at it all round. "Couldn't I give it too? From both of us?"

"No," said Pooh. "That would *not* be a good plan. Now I'll just wash it first, and then you can write on it."

Well, he washed the pot out, and dried it, while Owl licked the end of his pencil, and wondered how to spell "birthday."

10

"Can you read, Pooh?" he asked, a little anxiously. "There's a notice about knocking and ringing outside my door, which Christopher Robin wrote. Could you read it?"

"Christopher Robin told me what it said, and *then* I could."

"Well, I'll tell you what *this* says, and then you'll be able to."

So Owl wrote . . . and this is what he wrote:

HIPY PAPY BTHUTHDTH THUTHDA
BTHUTHDY.

Pooh looked on admiringly.

"I'm just saying 'A Happy Birthday,'" said Owl carelessly.

"It's a nice long one," said Pooh, very much impressed by it.

"Well, *actually*, of course, I'm saying 'A Very Happy Birthday with love from Pooh.' Naturally it takes a good deal of pencil to say a long thing like that."

"Oh, I see," said Pooh.

While all this was happening, Piglet had gone back to his own house to get Eeyore's balloon. He held it very tightly against himself, so that it shouldn't blow away, and he ran as fast as he could so as to get to Eeyore before Pooh did; for he thought that he would like to be the first one to give a present, just as if he had thought of it without being told by anybody.

And running along, and thinking how pleased Eeyore would be, he didn't look where he was going . . . and suddenly he put his foot in a rabbit hole, and fell down flat on his face.

BANG!!!???***!!!

Piglet lay there, wondering what had happened. At first he thought that the whole world had blown up; and then he thought that perhaps only the Forest part of it had; and then he thought that perhaps only *he* had, and he was now alone in the moon or somewhere, and would never see Christopher Robin or Pooh or Eeyore again. And then he thought, "Well, even if I'm in the moon, I needn't be face downwards all the time," so he got cautiously up and looked about him.

He was still in the Forest!

"Well, that's funny," he thought. "I wonder what that bang was. I couldn't have made such a noise just falling down. And where's my balloon? And what's that small piece of damp rag doing?"

It was the balloon!

"Oh, dear!" said Piglet. "Oh, dear, oh, dearie, dearie, dear! Well, it's too late now. I can't go back, and I haven't another balloon, and perhaps Eeyore doesn't *like* balloons so *very* much."

So he trotted on, rather sadly now, and down he came to the side of the stream where Eeyore was, and called out to him.

"Good morning, Eeyore," shouted Piglet.

"Good morning, Little Piglet," said Eeyore. "If it *is* a good morning," he said. "Which I doubt," said he. "Not that it matters," he said.

"Many happy returns of the day," said Piglet, having now got closer.

Eeyore stopped looking at himself in the stream, and turned to stare at Piglet.

"Just say that again," he said.

"Many hap———"

"Wait a moment."

Balancing on three legs, he began to bring his fourth leg very cautiously up to his ear. "I did this yesterday," he explained, as he fell down for the third time. "It's quite easy. It's so as I can hear better. . . . There, that's done it! Now then, what were you saying?" He pushed his ear forward with his hoof.

"Many happy returns of the day," said Piglet again.

"Meaning me?"

"Of course, Eeyore."

"My birthday?"

"Yes."

"Me having a real birthday?"

"Yes, Eeyore, and I've brought you a present."

Eeyore took down his right hoof from his right ear, turned round, and with great difficulty put up his left hoof.

12

"I must have that in the other ear," he said. "Now then."

"A present," said Piglet very loudly.

"Meaning me again?"

"Yes."

"My birthday still?"

"Of course, Eeyore."

"Me going on having a real birthday?"

"Yes, Eeyore, and I brought you a balloon."

"*Balloon?*" said Eeyore. "You did say balloon? One of those big coloured things you blow up? Gaiety, song-and-dance, here we are and there we are?"

"Yes, but I'm afraid—I'm very sorry, Eeyore —but when I was running along to bring it to you, I fell down."

"Dear, dear, how unlucky! You ran too fast, I expect. You didn't hurt yourself, Little Piglet?"

"No, but I—I—oh, Eeyore, I burst the balloon!" There was a very long silence.

"My balloon?" said Eeyore at last.

Piglet nodded.

"My birthday balloon?"

"Yes, Eeyore," said Piglet sniffing a little. "Here it is. With—with many happy returns of the day." And he gave Eeyore the small piece of damp rag.

"Is this it?" said Eeyore, a little surprised.

Piglet nodded.

"My present?"

Piglet nodded again.

"The balloon?"

"Yes."

"Thank you, Piglet," said Eeyore. "You don't mind my asking," he went on, "but what colour was this balloon when it—when it *was* a balloon?"

"Red."

"I just wondered. . . . Red," he murmured to himself. "My favourite colour. . . . How big was it?"

"About as big as me."

"I just wondered. . . . About as big as Piglet," he said to himself sadly. "My favourite size. Well, well."

Piglet felt very miserable, and didn't know what to say. He was still opening his mouth to begin something, and then deciding that it wasn't any good saying *that*, when he heard a shout from the other side of the river, and there was Pooh.

"Many happy returns of the day," called out Pooh, forgetting that he had said it already.

"Thank you, Pooh, I'm having them," said Eeyore gloomily.

"I've brought you a little present," said Pooh excitedly.

"I've had it," said Eeyore.

Pooh had now splashed across the stream to Eeyore, and Piglet was sitting a little way off, his head in his paws, snuffling to himself.

"It's a Useful Pot," said Pooh. "Here it is. And it's got 'A Very Happy Birthday with love from Pooh' written on it. That's what all that writing is. And it's for putting things in. There!"

When Eeyore saw the pot, he became quite excited.

"Why!" he said. "I believe my Balloon will just go into that Pot!"

"Oh, no, Eeyore," said Pooh. "Balloons are much too big to go into Pots. What you do with a balloon is, you hold the balloon————"

"Not mine," said Eeyore proudly. "Look, Piglet!" And as Piglet looked sorrowfully round, Eeyore picked the balloon up with his teeth, and placed it carefully in the pot; picked it out and put it on the ground; and then picked it up again and put it carefully back.

"So it does!" said Pooh. "It goes in!"

"So it does!" said Piglet. "And it comes out!"

"Doesn't it?" said Eeyore. "It goes in and out like anything."

"I'm very glad," said Pooh happily, "that I thought of giving you a Useful Pot to put things in."

"I'm very glad," said Piglet happily, "that I thought of giving you Something to put in a Useful Pot."

But Eeyore wasn't listening. He was taking the balloon out, and putting it back again, as happy as could be. . . .

Winnie-the-Pooh and
The Unbouncing of Tigger

One day *Rabbit and Piglet* were sitting outside Pooh's front door listening to Rabbit, and Pooh was sitting with them.

"In fact," said Rabbit, coming to the end of it at last, "Tigger's getting so Bouncy nowadays that it's time we taught him a lesson. Don't you think so, Piglet?"

Piglet said that Tigger *was* very Bouncy, and that if they could think of a way of unbouncing him, it would be a Very Good Idea.

"Well, I've got an idea," said Rabbit, "and here it is. We take Tigger for a long explore, somewhere where he's never been, and we lose him there, and next morning we find him again, and—mark my words—he'll be a different Tigger altogether."

The next day was quite a different day. Instead of being hot and sunny, it was cold and misty.

At first Pooh and Rabbit and Piglet walked together, and Tigger ran round them in circles, and then, when the path got narrower,

Tigger ran up and down in front of them, and then when you thought he wasn't there, there he was again, saying "I say, come on," and before you could say anything, there he wasn't.

Rabbit turned round and nudged Piglet. "The next time," he said. "Tell Pooh."

Tigger appeared suddenly, bounced into Rabbit, and disappeared again. "Now!" said Rabbit. He jumped into a hollow by the side

of the path, and Pooh and Piglet jumped after him. They crouched in the bracken, listening. The Forest was very silent when you stopped and listened to it.

"Where are you?" called Tigger.

There was a moment's silence, and then they heard him pattering off again. For a little longer they waited, until the Forest had become so still that it almost frightened them, and then Rabbit got up and stretched himself.

"Well?" he whispered proudly. "There we are! Just as I said."

"I've been thinking," said Pooh, "and I think—"

"No," said Rabbit. "Don't. Run. Come on." And they all hurried off, Rabbit leading the way.

"Lucky we know the Forest so well, or we might get lost," said Rabbit half an hour later, and he gave the careless laugh which you give when you know the Forest so well that you can't get lost.

Piglet sidled up to Pooh from behind.

"Pooh!" he whispered.

"Yes, Piglet?"

"Nothing," said Piglet, taking Pooh's paw. "I just wanted to be sure of you."

When Tigger had finished waiting for the others to catch him up, and they hadn't, and

when he had got tired of having nobody to say, "I say, come on" to, he thought he would go home. So he trotted back; and the first thing Kanga said when she saw him was "There's a good Tigger. You're just in time for your Strengthening Medicine," and she poured it out for him.

And it was just as they were finishing dinner that Christopher Robin put his head in at the door.

"Where's Pooh?" he asked.

"Tigger dear, where's Pooh?" said Kanga. Tigger explained what had happened at the same time that Roo was explaining about his Biscuit Cough and Kanga was telling them not both to talk at once, so it was some time before Christopher Robin guessed that Pooh and Piglet and Rabbit were all lost in the mist on the top of the Forest.

"Well," said Christopher Robin, "we shall have to go and find them, that's all. Come on, Tigger."

"The fact is," said Rabbit, "we've missed our way somehow."

"How would it be," said Pooh slowly, "if, as soon as we're out of sight of this Pit, we try to find it again?"

"I don't see much sense in that," said

"Try," said Piglet suddenly. "We'll wait here for you."

Rabbit gave a laugh to show how silly Piglet was, and walked into the mist. After he had gone a hundred yards, he turned and walked back again . . . and after Pooh and Piglet had waited twenty minutes for him, Pooh got up.

"I just thought," said Pooh. "Now then, Piglet, let's go home."

"But, Pooh," cried Piglet, all excited, "do you know the way?"

"No," said Pooh. "But there are twelve pots of honey in my cupboard, and they've been calling to me for hours. I couldn't hear them properly before, because Rabbit *would* talk, but if nobody says anything except those twelve pots, I *think*, Piglet, I shall know where they're calling from. Come on."

They walked off together; and for a long time Piglet said nothing, so as not to interrupt the pots; and just when he was getting so sure of himself that it didn't matter whether the pots went on calling or not, there was a shout from in front of them, and out of the mist came Christopher Robin.

Rabbit. "If I walked away from this Pit, and then walked back to it, of *course* I should find it."

"Oh, there you are," said Christopher Robin carelessly, trying to pretend that he hadn't been Anxious.

"Here we are," said Pooh.

"Where's Rabbit?"

"I don't know," said Pooh.

"Oh—well, I expect Tigger will find him. He's sort of looking for you all."

"Well," said Pooh, "I've got to go home for something, and so has Piglet, because we haven't had it yet, and—"

"I'll come and watch you," said Christopher Robin.

So he went home with Pooh, and watched him for quite a long time . . . and all the time he was watching, Tigger was tearing round the Forest making loud yapping noises for Rabbit. And at last a very Small and

24

Sorry Rabbit heard him. And the Small and Sorry Rabbit rushed through the mist at the noise, and it suddenly turned into Tigger; a Friendly Tigger, a Grand Tigger, a Large and Helpful Tigger, a Tigger who bounced, if he bounced at all, in just the beautiful way a Tigger ought to bounce.

"Oh, Tigger, I *am* glad to see you," cried Rabbit.

The Case of the
Light-Fingered Fiddler

"*It's a disgrace!*" exploded Pongo, the Dalmatian dog.

"What's a disgrace, Papa?" asked Lucky Puppy.

Pongo glared at the newspaper which was spread out on the floor of his dog house. "The royal jewels are missing!" he said. "It's all here in the paper. Yesterday the jewels were sent out to be cleaned. There were emerald rings, a sapphire necklace, ruby bracelets, a diamond tiara, and enough pearls for the world's biggest marble game. On the way to the jeweler's, they were stolen. There's no sign of them! Scotland Yard is baffled! It's a disgrace, that's what it is! It's an affront to every decent Englishman."

"And every English dog," put in Lucky, helpfully.

"Right!" agreed Pongo. His tail thumped impatiently on the floor. "We should do something about it," he said firmly. "We dogs, I mean. We have ways of knowing things that our humans. . . ." He left the sentence unfinished. Then he said, "The Twilight Bark! That's it! We'll rally all the dogs in England!"

So, that evening, the dogs in London were alerted. A Kerry in Kensington heard Pongo's message and passed it along. A St. Bernard in Bayswater, a spaniel in Soho, and a collie from Chelsea helped spread the word.

News of the missing jewels was passed from the dogs in the city to dogs in the outlying villages until, at last, the Twilight Bark came to the shaggy ear of an old sheep dog known as the Colonel. With the Colonel was his trusted friend, a lean and lively cat named Sergeant Tibs.

"What's that?" exclaimed the Colonel. He cocked his good ear. "Loyal fools?"

"Royal jewels, I think, sir," said Tibs respectfully. "Yes, three short barks and one long. Royal jewels. Pongo's sent word from London that we're to keep alert for signs of the scoundrels who took the royal jewels."

"Good show!" huffed the Colonel. "Obviously I'll be in charge of this area. Tibs, we must set up a headquarters, organize a staff, establish an officer's club. . . ."

Sergeant Tibs interrupted. "Hadn't we better concentrate on looking for the jewels, sir?"

"Yes, yes! All in good time. But first things first. I think Hell Hall would be a logical command post."

Sergeant Tibs shuddered. "That scary old place?"

"Why not? It's been empty since that awful Cruella de Vil woman moved out. Let's get over and inspect it."

Tibs wasn't too pleased at the idea, but he followed the Colonel out of their warm, cozy stable and across the fields toward the run-down mansion called Hell Hall.

As they approached the old manor house, however, they went more carefully, for there were lights in some of the windows.

"Odd!" muttered the Colonel. "The place is supposed to be vacant!"

An eerie sound floated from the house—a sound like wind moaning in the trees, and yet not like that at all.

Moving like shadows, the dog and the cat crept up to a lighted window. Sergeant Tibs leaped to the Colonel's back. The Colonel raised his head and looked in through the dusty panes of glass.

" 'Pon my word!" gasped the Colonel.

For inside the house were their old enemies, the villainous Badun brothers, Horace and Jasper.

There was a third man with the Baduns—a tall, thin, scarecrow of a man with a pointed, bald head and the nose of a vulture. He was sitting on a high stool playing a bass violin. A melancholy voom-voom-voom filled the air as he drew a heavy bow across the strings. On the floor near his feet was a big case for the violin.

Tibs and the Colonel retreated to the end of the garden.

"Something's up, Tibs!" announced the Colonel. "Mark my words, where those Baduns are, there's trouble!"

Tibs was about to agree when, suddenly, the sound of the bass violin was stilled. Moments later the tall, bald man and the Baduns left the house, got into a car, and drove away.

"Now's our chance!" cried Sergeant Tibs, scampering toward the back door.

The door was ajar. The Colonel nosed it open, and Tibs flashed through and began sniffing around. The violin case seemed interesting. It looked too big even for the huge bass fiddle.

"Colonel, sir," said Tibs. "I think this has a false bottom."

"Yes, yes!" scoffed the Colonel. "It's to carry music in."

"Music—or stolen jewels?" suggested Tibs.

The Colonel nodded. "I was just about to think of that."

Tibs prodded the case with his paw. "If there *were* jewels here, they aren't here now," he announced. "I suggest we search the premises thoroughly."

"Good show. Carry on!" ordered the Colonel.

They went all through the house. When they got to the cellar they found footprints leading across the dirt floor to a door which was bolted, chained, and padlocked.

"I think we should see what's behind that door, sir," said Tibs.

"Carry on," said the Colonel.

"But how, sir?" asked Tibs.

"Good heavens, Tibs!" huffed the Colonel. "Do I have to think of every little detail?"

"If I might suggest, sir," said Tibs soothingly, "we can send word back to London by the Twilight Bark and get Pongo here. He'll know what to do."

"Just what I was about to say, Sergeant!" replied the Colonel. And they slipped out of the house and ran to send for Pongo.

It was late the next day when Pongo arrived. He had Lucky Puppy in tow. The Colonel glared at the Dalmatian pup. "What's this raw recruit doing here?" he demanded.

Pongo replied airily, "It will be good training for him."

So the four of them—the Colonel, Tibs, Pongo, and Lucky—went warily across the fields to Hell Hall. Outside the library window they stopped and listened. Horace and Jasper Badun were inside, talking.

"I can't stand that bloomin' scratchin' on the fiddle!" Horace was saying.

"Aw, but all great geniuses have their little quirks," Jasper countered. "Besides, Sherlock Holmes fiddled. Einstein fiddled. Why can't the Fiddler fiddle?"

The droning of the bass violin went on and on. Pongo beckoned the others away from the window and led them toward the back of the house, and the open kitchen door. Hardly breathing, they made their way into the house and down to the cellar.

"We're safe for a while," said Pongo. "The Baduns are busy arguing. And as long as we can hear the bass violin playing upstairs, we know the Fiddler won't bother us. Let's get busy."

The locked door which had so dismayed the Colonel was no problem at all to Pongo. The Dalmatian started tunneling under it, digging away the soft earth of the cellar floor.

Before long, Lucky Puppy piped up. "That tunnel's big enough for me now, Papa," he said. "I can get through there."

Pongo backed away from the door. "Okay, son. Crawl inside and see what you can see."

The Colonel, Tibs, and Pongo waited,

listening to the voom-voom of the bass violin. Lucky Puppy wriggled under the door.

A moment later Lucky called, "There are some big funny marbles in here!"

"Marbles?" echoed the Colonel.

Lucky appeared again in the tunnel. There was an emerald the size of an egg gripped in his jaws, and a platinum bracelet was wrapped around his neck.

"The royal jewels!" exclaimed Pongo.

"Good show! We've found them!" said the Colonel. "Don't forget to put that on the morning report, Sergeant."

Pongo immediately took charge. "I'll go to the village for the police," he said. "I know how to get them out here right away. Lucky, you put the jewels back behind the door so the police will find them all together. Then all of you leave! Don't stay here in the house."

Lucky disappeared behind the door, and Pongo ran up the stairs toward the kitchen. The Colonel and Tibs remained on guard. Upstairs, the voom-voom of the violin continued.

"I say, Lucky," growled the Colonel. "Do hurry up."

Just then, complete quiet enveloped Hell Hall.

"Come on, Lucky," whispered Sergeant Tibs nervously. "Let's get out of here!"

The cellar door was swung wide and the two Baduns loomed large at the top of the steps. "Wha . . . ?" cried Horace. "A dog!"

"And a cat!" yelled Jasper.

Tibs and the Colonel scrambled up onto a packing crate and then out through an open window. They streaked away toward the bushes that edged the field.

Only there, in the safety of the sheltering branches, did they stop. For once, words failed the Colonel. They had succeeded in finding the royal jewels, but they had failed, too. Lucky was trapped in the locked room in that horrible old house. Poor little Lucky. He was at the mercy of the Baduns and that criminal genius, the Fiddler!

"We must rescue young Lucky from the Baduns and the Fiddler!" the Colonel announced. The old sheep dog was pacing his command post at the edge of the field.

Sergeant Tibs agreed. "Let's go!" he urged.

"Not so fast, Sergeant! This is a military operation! We've got to plan our campaign!"

Tibs saluted.

"We must have a meeting of the general staff," the Colonel pointed out. "We've got to plan strategy, send out patrols, have the ladies' auxiliary stand by with coffee and donuts, prepare . . . "

Tibs knew only too well that the Colonel's planning session might last longer than Lucky Puppy's luck, so he innocently reminded the Colonel of his famous campaign at the Battle of Waterpup.

"A great victory!" the Colonel exclaimed. "Er . . . what did I do?"

"You attacked from all sides and so confused the enemy that they were helpless when the reinforcements arrived!"

"Of course!" The Colonel thought for a moment. Then, "Tibs, I have a plan," he announced. "I will remain here at my command post. You will attack from all sides and so confuse the enemy that. . . ."

Before he had finished, Tibs was racing toward the fearful house known as Hell Hall.

Meanwhile, Pongo had reached the village and set up a howl that brought every dog in town hurrying to meet him. He quickly explained that they must help lead the police to Hell Hall, where the jewel thieves were hiding.

A dachshund spoke up. "What if the police don't understand what we want them to do?"

"Do whatever you must," Pongo instructed, "but get the police to Hell Hall."

Immediately the dogs fanned out through the village streets. The dachshund found a man in blue, then began nipping at his heels. A cocker spaniel pushed over a coal scuttle practically under the nose of another officer. A French poodle sought out the Chief Constable himself. She fluttered her long, silky eyelashes at him, then bit him lightly on the ankle to make sure he got the message. He chased her down the street to the village square, where he found himself face to face with the rest of his force. The police were all surrounded by happily barking dogs.

Suddenly the other dogs were silent. Only Pongo barked and jumped and growled and snapped. Then he stood absolutely still and deliberately raised one paw to point down the road toward Hell Hall.

The Chief Constable shook his head with wonder. "Men," he said, "I do believe these dogs are trying to tell us something."

At that, the dogs broke into delighted barks of agreement and raced down the road. After a moment of hesitation, the mystified policemen followed them.

While Pongo had been busy getting the police, Sergeant Tibs hadn't been idle. The intrepid cat had crept back into the frightening old house. Sure enough, the Baduns were there trying to work the rusty padlock on the door of the basement room where Lucky was trapped. Tibs surveyed the situation for

a second, then dashed in to claw Horace's ankle and bite Jasper on the knee.

The two evildoers howled with pain and rage. Jasper reached for Tibs, but the cat streaked away across the room and leaped onto a work bench. From there he scrambled up onto a stack of fruit baskets. From the top of the baskets he launched himself onto Horace's back, claws exposed.

"Get this crazy cat off me!" cried Horace.

Jasper swung at Tibs with a large stick just as the cat jumped to the floor. Unfortunately for Horace, Jasper's aim was very good. The stick landed squarely between Horace's sixth vertebra and his fourth cat-scratch!

"Not me, you fool!" Horace raged. "Hit the *cat!*"

But Tibs was already launching a new offensive. This time he overwhelmed Jasper with a barrage of spitting and snarling. Each time one of the thieves tried to get away, the Sergeant attacked again, chasing the Baduns in circles, squares, ovals, oblongs, and patterns of helpless confusion.

"Help!" Jasper yelled at last. "Someone— HELP!"

The words were hardly out of Jasper's mouth before the front door of the house burst open and a small army of policemen, accompanied by Pongo, the Colonel, and all the village dogs, came charging down the cellar stairs. Sergeant Tibs smiled and retreated from the field of combat to lick his whiskers in triumph.

"What's going on here?" the Chief Constable demanded.

"Oh, nothing," the Baduns replied, trying to hide their surprise and fear. "Uh— just a little game."

But Pongo was already posed with one paw pointing to the locked door. "Help me!" he called to the other dogs. "We have to make the policemen understand where the stolen jewels are hidden!"

The other dogs quickly followed Pongo's example. Even the Colonel did his bit, though he wasn't very athletic and he fell over twice before the Chief Constable got the idea.

When the police forced the lock and the door swung open, there was Lucky cheerfully playing with the world's largest pigeon-blood ruby.

"Lucky!" cried Pongo, trying to be stern. "You should have more respect for the royal jewels!"

"I thought it was a glass Easter egg," Lucky answered with an innocent smile. "Who are your friends, Papa?"

Before Pongo could explain that his friends were the police, the Chief Constable had seen the gems heaped under Lucky's paws and was snapping heavy-duty handcuffs on Horace and Jasper Badun.

The dogs were congratulating themselves on the capture of the thieves when Sergeant Tibs suddenly stopped and frowned. "There was a third thief," he whispered to Pongo. "The man who played the bass violin!"

Pongo was puzzled. "I don't know how we can tell the policemen about him," he told Tibs. "And I'll bet the Fiddler is the brains of the gang!"

"I say!" The Chief Constable, who had been sorting through the jewels, looked up with a very unhappy expression on his face. "The Star of Liverpool necklace is missing! It's the most valuable item of them all!"

It was then that Tibs remembered the Fiddler's big fiddle case! No doubt the Fiddler had hidden the necklace there, hoping to fool the Baduns and keep the necklace for himself.

Tibs dashed up the steps from the basement and crossed the hall to the room where he had first seen the fiddle case. Sure enough, there it was, lying open and empty on the floor. The cat nosed around the case, sniffing and snuffing. Then he stepped carefully into the case. There was something very strange here—something that . . .

What the brave cat did not know was that the evil man known as the Fiddler had hidden behind the kitchen cupboard when he heard the policemen thunder down to the basement. He had guessed that the stolen jewels had been discovered. Now he was stealing silently into the room where he had left his fiddle case. And . . .

WHOMP!

The cover of the case snapped shut, trapping Tibs inside! And a secret compartment snapped open, spilling a necklace of emeralds and moonstones about the cat's neck. A second later, Tibs fell against the side of the case as it was lifted from the floor.

"YEEE-OWWW!!"

Tibs rocked from side to side. He yeowled and yelled and screeched and spit. Cats hate to be cooped up in small places, and Sergeant Tibs was no exception. His voice was shrill with terror.

The Fiddler was taking a desperate chance. He had to be silent to steal through the house, collect his violin case, and escape without being seen by dog or man. When the pent-up cat began to snarl, the master criminal panicked. With the violin case bumping clumsily on the floor, the Fiddler ran for the hallway.

There in the doorway was Pongo staring at him. Behind Pongo were several large policemen, and they were staring at him, too. And to one side of the policemen were Horace and Jasper.

Before the Fiddler could say a word, the Chief Constable seized the violin case and opened it. Still complaining at the top of his voice, Tibs streaked out. Spitting and hissing, he glared at the Fiddler. The Star of Liverpool necklace was draped loosely over his ears.

Lucky Puppy padded forward and nuzzled Tibs in a friendly way. "The newspaper photographers are coming," warned Lucky. "Don't you want to take off the necklace before they take your picture? Who ever heard of a tomcat wearing emeralds?"

At this, Tibs *did* take off the necklace. Rather, he let the Chief Constable take it off. The police took the Fiddler and the Baduns to jail, and Tibs and the dogs had their pictures taken for the newspapers. Then the Colonel congratulated all the dogs for having done their duty. Lucky Puppy got a

very special commendation from the Colonel. Not only had he been the first to discover the jewels, but he had kept Sergeant Tibs from being a very embarrassed hero!

At last Pongo said it was time to start for home. Lucky Puppy was very pleased. "I'm glad we were proper, patriotic dogs and captured those thieves," he said to his father, "but it will be awfully nice to be back home with my own favorite dog blanket!"

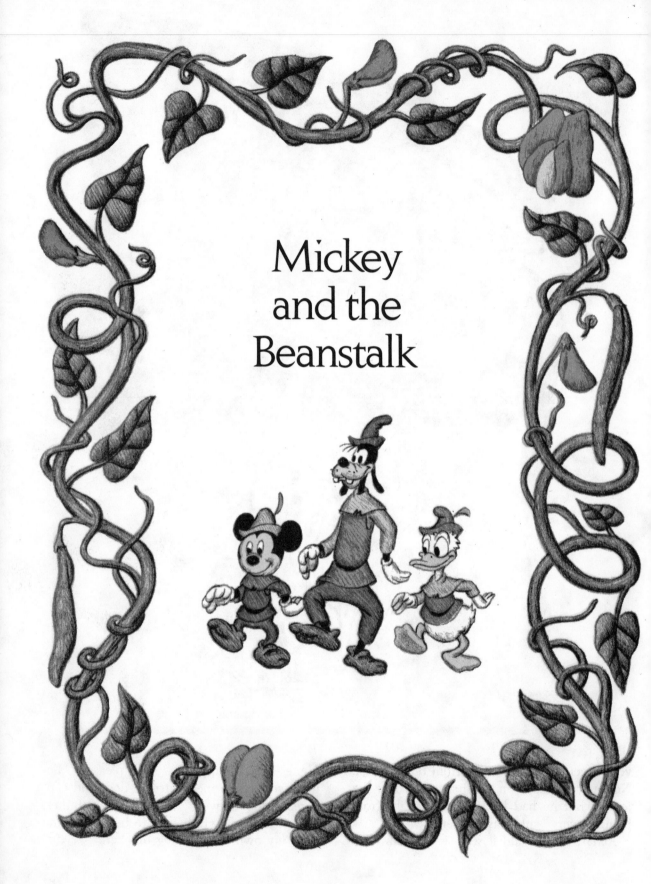

Mickey
and the
Beanstalk

There was once a most beautiful valley. Rolling hills stretched all around it, and a broad river flowed peacefully through it. There were green trees, quiet roads, and pleasant farms. And best of all, the air was always filled with laughter, so that far and wide this enchanted spot was known as Happy Valley.

Now the secret of the valley's enchantment was a magic singing harp. It was her songs, ringing out from a castle, which stood in the center of the valley, that cast the magic spell of happiness over the land.

But one day a giant shadow fell over the castle. And when the shadow lifted, the magic harp was gone.

With her went all the happiness of the valley. The crops withered away. The trees died. The river dried up and disappeared. And the people grew sadder and hungrier day by day.

In one little home in the valley lived three friends—Mickey, Donald, and Goofy by name. Once they had been happy and prosperous

farmers, with plenty of good food on their tables. Now they were down to their last crust of bread and their one last bean!

What could they do, they asked themselves over and over again, to keep from starving? To be sure, they still owned one cow, but she was such an old and faithful friend, they knew they could never eat her.

"We could sell the cow," suggested Mickey.

"It is the only way," the others agreed.

So off to market trudged Mickey with the faithful cow.

At home, while they waited, Goofy and Donald prepared for a great feast. They got out their biggest roasting pans and platters, their spices and seasonings, and recipe books.

Then back came Mickey from market. In a little box he carried the payment he had received for the cow—not steaks or roasts or chops, not even a soupbone, but beans!

"Beans!" screamed Donald.

"Beans!" groaned Goofy.

"But, fellows," Mickey tried to explain,

"these are magic beans. If you plant them by the light of a full moon, you get—"

"More beans!" Donald broke in, and he hurled the beans to the floor, where they rolled through a knothole and disappeared.

That was a black moment for the three friends. They trudged gloomily off to bed, supperless and sad.

But as the three friends slept, and just when everything looked darkest, in through the window came a ray of light. It was moonlight—the light of a full moon! And a silvery beam shone down through the knothole where the magic beans had fallen.

It was just as Mickey had promised. Under the spell of the moonlight those magic beans

sprouted and grew. First up through the knothole curled a slender sprout. But it did not stop there. Higher and higher it climbed, while the three friends slept on.

Thicker and stronger and taller grew the magic beanstalk until it began to lift that little house up from the desolate valley—up, up, up to a magic land above the clouds.

So it happened that when morning dawned, the three friends looked out, not upon the dismal, dried-up ruin of Happy Valley, but upon the strange and wonderful landscape of this land in the sky.

In the distance gleamed a huge castle.

"Hey, fellows!" cried Goofy, who woke first and was the first to look out the window. "See what I found. A castle—a castle in the sky!"

"Gee!" cried Donald, scrambling up beside him for a look. "Maybe there's food there!"

"Let's go and see!" said Mickey.

So off trudged the three friends. The castle was farther away than it looked. They walked and walked through a giant land. Giant grasses and flowers towered above their heads. Giant caterpillars humped along the forest paths. There were giant footprints, too, but our friends did not stop to worry about those.

At last only a wide moat separated them from the castle. Mickey found a giant pea pod which made them a splendid boat, and away they rowed, straight up to the castle's forbidding walls.

Then up a long stairway of stone they clambered, until at last they found themselves in the castle itself. And there before them was the answer to their dreams—a huge table loaded down with wonderful things to eat!

It was a truly giant-sized table, as tall as a young mountain. But that could not stop those hungry searchers now. Up the towering legs they scrambled and then, without a moment wasted, they began to feast upon the huge cheeses, the mounds of great, green peas, the bowlfuls and jarfuls and platefuls of all sorts and flavors of food!

But wait. What was this? Through an open doorway they heard the thud of giant footsteps. And they heard a big voice singing—

"Fee-fi-fo-fum!
He-hi-ho-hum!
I'm a most amazing guy,
A most amazing guy am I!"

The next moment, there in the doorway stood the owner of the castle, Willie the giant. What made him an amazing guy, they learned from the rest of his song, was that he could change himself into any shape he chose.

Donald and Goofy trembled as they listened to the giant's song. They did not care to see the giant's other shapes; they raced away to hide. But Mickey was watching the giant's shadow. It was the same huge shadow that had fallen over Happy Valley the day the magic harp disappeared!

Mickey had just time to scuttle under a folded napkin as Willie pulled his big chair up to the big table and sat down to eat.

"Yum, yum," said Willie happily. "Pot roast —chocolate pot roast, with green gravy!"

He picked up his napkin—and there was Mickey! Mickey ran for shelter, but Willie had seen him. A giant hand pounced, and Mickey was trapped.

"Of course, if you can't do a fly—" Mickey suggested.

"Oh, all right!" said Willie sulkily. "A teeny-eeny fly, with pink wings!"

Then, while Willie muttered his magic words, out came Goofy and Donald, and with Mickey they seized the handle of the big fly swatter, ready for one big swat!

But Willie fooled them. He turned into a huge bunny with pink ears. And when he

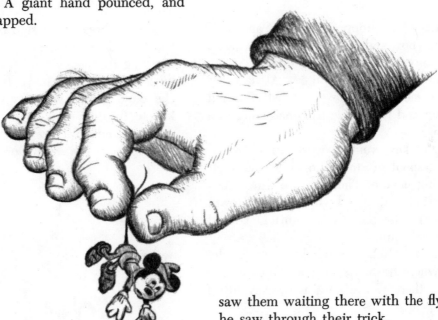

"Ho, ho!" laughed the giant, holding up his small prisoner. "Where do you think you're going?"

Mickey thought fast.

"Is it really true," he said admiringly, "that you can change yourself into anything?"

"Sure." Willie gave a giant giggle. "Go on, suggest something."

"Anything?" said Mickey, eyeing a huge fly swatter.

"Sure, anything," said Willie.

"Well," said Mickey, thinking hard, "could you change into a—well, a fly?"

Willie was disappointed. "Aw, you don't want a fly!" he said. "How about a bunny with long pink ears?"

saw them waiting there with the fly swatter, he saw through their trick.

"Hey!" he roared. "Are you trying to fool Willie? I'll fix you!"

And he snatched them all up in his great big fist.

"I'll fix you," he muttered again, "but first I want my dinner and some music."

And Willie unlocked a box on a high shelf and pulled out the missing magic harp of Happy Valley!

"Miss Harp!" cried Goofy. But before he had time to say any more, he found himself being tossed, with his friends, down into that same dark box, and he heard the clank of the key as the giant locked it up.

Then Willie dropped the key into his breast pocket and went back to his dinner, feeling well satisfied with himself. He did not guess

that Mickey had dropped down, by accident, behind the box, and was hiding there, waiting for a chance to rescue his friends.

Mickey waited and waited. At last his chance came—when the giant had finished his dinner and the magic harp had sung him to sleep.

Then Mickey went to work. First he anchored a spool of stout thread to the shelf with a big needle. Then, as the thread unwound, Mickey dropped with it, down, down, down toward the giant's chest, until he landed with a small thud.

On tiptoe Mickey padded across to the pocket where he had seen the giant put the key. Yes, there it was! But as Mickey lifted

the key, the giant's snuffbox flew open, and Mickey breathed in a great gulp of the nose-tickling stuff!

"Ka-ka-tchoo!" The whole pocket shivered under Mickey's sneeze.

Willie roused up at the sound and sniffed about. Then the snuff caught up with him, too.

"KA-KA-TCHOO!" he roared, while Mickey trembled.

But Willie only looked drowsily around the room, stretched once, and went back to sleep.

Mickey breathed a sigh of relief. Then up the thread he went again, hand over hand, carrying the heavy key. It took every bit of his strength to pull himself and the key over the edge of the shelf, and then to lift the key to the lock—and turn it!

It worked! Up flew the box lid, and out scrambled Goofy and Donald.

There was not a moment to lose. Down the thread they slid; then up to the table to rescue the harp and down again to the floor they raced.

Now they were really on their way, but Mickey had one last inspiration. He stopped to tie the giant's shoelaces together, to keep Willie from chasing them.

He was just in time, too, for Willie woke up as the three friends were running across the castle's great stone floor.

With a roar he lurched to his feet, swinging his club. But the shoelaces tripped him up, and he tumbled across the table.

With another roar he flung his club at Mickey.

"Whew!" cried Mickey, as he dodged the flying weapon. "That was too close for comfort!"

On they raced, and in another moment they had squeezed under the big outer door of the castle, while behind them Willie fumbled at his shoelaces.

Before they reached the top of the magic beanstalk, they could hear Willie's footsteps thudding behind them. He was on the trail again!

They practically fell down that beanstalk!

Down, down, down—and at last the parched earth of their home valley was under their feet once more.

Then Mickey snatched up an old saw and zizz, zizz, zizz they sawed through that thick beanstalk as fast as they could work. At last it cracked, it wavered, it swayed. Then, with a tremendous thud, it crashed down into the valley!

And high, high above, where the stalk had pierced the clouds, they could see Willie's angry, puzzled face peering down.

"'Bye, Willie!" shouted Mickey.

Then away they raced, to return the magic singing harp to the castle on the hill.

Soon the sweet notes of the harp's magic song rang out over the sad valley again. And the old enchantment was reborn. First a rain cloud came racing over the hills, and a warm shower fell upon the parched earth and set the dry river to bubbling once more. Then the sun shone, and the trees and grass sent out new little shoots of green. And soon the lovely sound of laughter filled the air once more in Happy Valley.

"Gosh," said Goofy, as the three friends stood in the doorway of their new home that evening, "it sure is fun to be happy!"

Adventures of the Brave Mice

In these stories, that fearless mouse, Jaq, who presently occupies the position of Chief Cheesetaster in Cinderella's royal palace, tells how he and his friend Gus became friends with the court magician, and how some most unusual adventures follow.

The Magic Cheese

It seems to me that not enough credit is given to mice for the great advances that have been made in the world. Now take me, for example. I'm a mouse. Pretty insignificant, some people would say. But if it hadn't been for me Columbus might never have discovered America.

Does this sound fantastic? Well, it is—but it's true, all the same.

It all started with Mandor, the official wizard at Cinderella's court. In case you didn't realize it, no royal court is really complete without a wizard or soothsayer, or at least a fortune teller. Mandor wasn't a very famous wizard, or even a very good one. As a matter of fact, hardly anyone believed in him. But he was there, tucked away high up in the north tower, with his bats and his books and his bottles and jars of strange things like newt's dust and mandrake root. Sometimes one of the maids would creep up the winding stairs and ask Mandor to mix a love potion for her. Mandor's love potions had a strange way of working out. They're still talking in the kitchen about the time the cook used one to . . . but that's another story.

One evening, Gus and I were having a little chat with Mandor when he brought up the subject of the enchanted cheese. "It's a wonderful cheese," he told us. "I've been saving it for years and years, waiting for a brave, adventurous spirit to try it. And you're both brave and adventurous spirits."

"What does the cheese do?" I asked. I must admit, I'm a little suspicious of cheese that anyone has been saving for years and years.

Mandor leaned closer to the table, where Gus and I were sitting on a large crock of mummy dust. "If you eat the cheese while I say an incantation, you'll be transported to any time and place you desire."

"Really?"

"Really!"

"You mean time-travel?"

"Absolutely."

"We could go back to the court of Cleopatra, for example?"

"Without a doubt."

"Or to China with Marco Polo?"

"Yes, indeed."

"Suppose you don't say the incantation right?"

Mandor looked pained and ran his hand through his beard, startling a bat that seemed to have taken up housekeeping there. "Of course I'll say the incantation right," he said. "I've been practicing every night for five years!"

"Hmmm." I thought about it for a minute. "How do we get back from the court of Cleopatra, or wherever we go?"

"That's the easiest part," Mandor assured us. "With the particular incantation I plan to use, the charm wears off after three days and you're back."

"You sure?" Gus squeaked.

"Don't worry about a thing." Mandor patted him on the back with one finger, nearly knocking him off the crock of mummy dust. "You're clever and resourceful mice, and that's why I've chosen you. Shall we try for ancient Egypt now?"

I remembered that the old Egyptians were very fond of cats and said, "How about China instead?"

"All right, all right. Just make sure you notice everything you see, and if you should happen to meet any magicians, try to find out something about their incantations. Those old Chinese magicians were the best."

Mandor doddered off to a big, deep cupboard that stood in one corner of the tower, took out a moldy, old cheese dish, and showed us the cheese. Surprisingly, it looked like very ordinary, yellow cheese.

"A crumb will be enough," Mandor said. "Hold it in your hand and when I stamp my left foot three times, eat it."

So we each held a crumb of cheese and Mandor stood in the middle of the room, spun around three times and said:

"Hum-didy, hibidy, hickory, doc!
Hi-didy, why-didy, mouse up the clock!"

Then he stamped his foot three times and we swallowed the cheese.

The next thing we knew, the tower was gone and we were sitting on the floor in one corner of a long, gray stone room. At the other end of the room were two big chairs, thrones really, with a red and gold canopy over them.

"This not look like China," Gus whispered.

Some men dressed in strange clothes, long stockings and short pants and funny coats, stood around near the thrones. Then a boy wearing a uniform or livery of some sort, obviously a page, blew a blast on a trumpet and yelled: "Their Majesties, King Ferdinand and Queen Isabella!"

Ferdinand and Isabella! That Mandor was some magician! He tried to send us to ancient Cathay, and we wind up in Spain in about 1490!

The men around the throne bowed and in came the king and queen. He wasn't much to look at, but she was pretty spectacular, dressed in a brilliant blue gown.

"The Italian sea captain, Senor Christoforo Columbo," yelled the page. And in he came, Chris Columbus himself, looking very much like his pictures in the history books.

Well, he bowed to their majesties and

started telling them about how the world was really round, not flat as everyone thought, and how by sailing west he could find a new trade route to the Indies and how wonderful it would be for their majesties to help such a noble venture and one thing and another. And let me tell you, he was just about the worst salesman I've ever heard. He couldn't have convinced me of anything—not anything! He droned on and on about ocean currents and shipping by sea rather than by land and cargo stowage and gross tonnage per cargo hold and every so often he would stretch out a big map of the world, or a globe, and show it to the king and queen. Isabella got more

and more bored and King Ferdinand simply went to sleep.

"He never gonna discover America that way," Gus remarked. I agreed.

At last, the audience was over and Columbus trailed himself out.

"C'mon," I said to Gus. "We've got to help."

That night, when Queen Isabella came into her chamber, there was a note on her dressing table next to her jewel box. It told her that Columbus would never discover a trade route to the Indies, but that he would find a great new continent—a "New Spain"—and that she would sell her jewels to buy ships for him, and pay a crew to man the ships.

notes for lunch and tea and dinner. Gus and I were getting writers' cramp. And all this while we had to watch out for the cat.

That's right! A cat! A big yellow tomcat who was very nippy on his feet. We were a little out of practice, because Cinderella didn't allow cats in *her* palace, so that big tom almost caught us a couple of times. Once Gus had to take refuge in a teapot and once I escaped the cat only by diving into the ornamental fountain in the royal garden and swimming underwater for quite some distance.

When the third day dawned, we knew our time was running out. Mandor's spell would wear off soon and Isabella still hadn't consented to outfit Columbus for his trip to the new world, even though the mysterious notes were beginning to make an impression on her.

It was time for desperate measures!

Columbus was to have another audience with their majesties at eleven, so Gus and I took up separate stations behind the portraits in the royal portrait gallery. We knew the queen would have to pass through the gallery

That's all the note said, but it was enough. The queen jumped up and screamed for the guards. She said that someone had gotten into the room to leave the note. They searched, and of course since they were looking for a person, they didn't ever think to peer up on top of the bed curtains where Gus and I were watching.

After things quieted down and the queen went to bed—and to sleep—I scooted down the bed curtains and pinned another note to her pillow. It was more of the same. In the morning when she woke up there was more screeching and scurrying and another scene with the guards.

And so it went for two days. Notes on the breakfast table, notes in the sewing basket,

on her way to see Columbus in the throne room.

Promptly at eleven, she came. And that dratted cat was following her. But cat or no cat, we did our duty.

As she passed the portrait of King Ferdinand's great-great uncle on his mother's side, Gus yelled out, "You'll be the greatest queen in history if you help Columbus."

Isabella stopped dead and stared at the portrait. And the cat went up to the wall and sniffed very suspiciously under the picture. At that moment, from behind the painting of King Ferdinand's father, I called, "Sell your jewels and you'll be famous forever."

She whirled around and ran over to my hiding place, the cat just behind her, and Gus quickly scampered to the portrait of Isabella's grandmother's brother, a dark gentleman with a large beard. Just as the queen reached my side of the room, Gus called out once more. We kept this up with the cat and the queen both getting more and more frantic until we heard the voice of the page in the throne room. He was announcing the arrival of Columbus. The queen put her hands up to her head, looked around rather wildly at the pictures and said, "All right! All right! I'll do it." And she ran into the throne room.

"Hooray!" cheered Gus, and he fell out from behind a very bad picture of Isabella's uncle.

The cat saw him and started to leap.

"Look out!" I squeaked.

At that exact instant, the portrait gallery wavered and shimmered and grew dim. The cat faded, in mid-leap, and Gus and I were back in the tower with old Mandor. The spell had worn off in the nick of time!

Mandor was very disappointed when he heard where we'd been. "I can't understand it," he kept saying. "That spell was just right to send you to China. Maybe I need more practice."

"Never mind, Mandor," I told him. "The spell was a dilly."

And it was. Because without Mandor's spell and the efforts of two brave mice, would Columbus ever have discovered America?

The Vegetarian Cat

No one has ever accused Gus of being brilliant. He's just not the smartest mouse who ever came down the pike. But still, there's a certain common horse sense, or should I say mouse sense, about Gus. And he's always been perfectly sound on the subject of cats. Leave them alone is Gus's motto, and he acts on it. You'd never find Gus loitering in the near neighborhood of a cat.

That's why it was such a shock to me when I strolled into Mandor's tower room one night to visit the old magician and discovered Gus and Mandor tenderly feeding cream to a small, wet, bedraggled kitten. I thought Gus had actually flipped. I mean, have you ever heard of a mouse being nice to a cat? It's absolutely unnatural.

But when Gus explained the situation, it began to make sense in a weird sort of way. Well, no, it didn't really make sense, but at least I could understand why Gus was behaving so strangely. It seems the whole idea was dreamed up by Annie Churchmouse.

I should explain that Annie is far and away the silliest mouse in the entire kingdom. She went high-society on us shortly after we all moved into the palace. She changed her name to Antoinette de l'Eglise and took to wearing brocade gowns and a powdered wig. Have you ever seen a mouse in a powdered wig? Looks pretty ridiculous.

To make a long story short, Annie had found the kitten next to the palace moat. Evidently someone had tried to drown it, but the kitten had managed to crawl out of the moat because it was wet and miserable. Instead of removing herself rapidly from the area, Annie somehow got the bubble-brained idea that the kitten was a "poor little thing" and it should be helped. Now, only a mouse with a complete vacuum between the ears could ever think of such a thing, but Annie thought of it. She whipped off and got Gus and made him promise that he would per-suade Mandor to shelter and feed the cat. Gus tried to argue with her, but of course he lost. There isn't a mouse in the palace who doesn't outweigh Gus in the argument department. The upshot of it all was that Gus *did* give his solemn word that he would help take care of the cat.

Fortunately, the cat was harmless enough then. Just a ball of fur that could hardly creep around. But I shuddered to think of what would happen when it got a little older, and Gus shuddered with me.

"Don't worry," Mandor said.

"Don't worry?" moaned Gus. "Annie make me promise I take care of cat. She say it cruel to hurt kitten."

Mandor put on the wise expression he uses when he concocts wart cures or performs important incantations. "Suppose," he said thoughtfully, "just suppose you never fed the cat meat. Suppose you raised it to be a vegetarian and to eat eggs and milk and cheese and vegetables. It stands to reason that the cat would never become a ' mouser.' "

I shuddered again at the thought. But I had to admit that Mandor was making sense.

We took Mandor's advice. We fed that cat milk and cream, and later cottage cheese and cooked vegetables with a little cod liver oil thrown in for good measure. Mandor insisted that all growing youngsters needed cod liver oil. And it worked! The cat rewarded us by growing into the most gentle of creatures. I suppose he regarded himself as an honorary mouse. He never mewed; he squeaked instead. And he loved to join in the games the young mice played on the rooftops or in the palace courtyard. He never even minded being "it" for a round of "Bell the Cat."

I must admit he was ugly. I mean, how often do you see a cat with black and gray and white *and* orange stripes. He was bow-legged, too, and rolled from side to side when he walked, like a salty old pirate. But it wasn't so much his coloring or his bowed legs that were disturbing. It was something about

his face. That cat had a crooked smile and a fixed way of staring at you with his big green eyes that made timid folks more than somewhat nervous. He looked like a cat that *knew* things, if you get what I mean. He looked like a cat that could peer into your mind and tell what you were thinking.

I tried hard, but I never really got used to him. It always gave me a terrible start to look up and see him peering at me. But Gus became very fond of him. He spent a great deal of time rolling a crumpled ball of paper around for the cat to chase and brushing the cat's fur with a very nice, stiff little doll's hairbrush he'd found somewhere that was just perfect for the purpose.

One night, when the cat was about six months old, Mandor came across a crumbling scrap of paper in one of his old magic books. It may have been slipped between the pages years before—perhaps when Mandor was a struggling young student at the State College of Wizards. At any rate, Mandor became pretty excited when he found this paper.

"The formula for alchemy," he yelled. "I'd forgotten I had it!"

How typical of Mandor, I thought, to forget he had the formula for alchemy, whatever alchemy is.

"What's alchemy?" asked Gus, who was scratching the cat behind the ears.

"Why, it's the secret of making gold out of lead," said Mandor, his eyes gleaming. "It's one of the oldest magic formulas in the world. It can make me rich as Solomon."

"How do you use the formula, Mandor?" I asked. I was only mildly excited. Mandor's formulas have a way of not turning out as advertised.

Mandor consulted his scrap of paper. "First you heat some lead in a crucible," he said. He looked around for his crucible and discovered that the cat was eating supper from it.

"Well, I suppose a saucepan will do as well," he said. "It isn't really important. Then, when the lead has melted, you put in some simple sulphur and a bit of philosopher's stone and . . . uh, oh!"

Mandor's face fell.

"No philosopher's stone?" Gus asked politely.

"No philosopher's stone," Mandor admitted.

"What's a philosopher's stone?"

"It's a magic stone," Mandor explained. "My old professor at the College used to have one. It was handy for all sorts of things—like curing headaches, predicting weather, making gold. And it was a good doorstop. It's an absolute necessity for an alchemist. You've just got to have a philosopher's stone."

Poor Mandor. We went off to bed and left him there, muttering and mumbling about the philosopher's stone and leafing through old, dog-eared books. But early the next morning, before Gus and I were out of bed, there was a terrific knocking on the wall of our apartment. We looked out into the pink throne room through the hole that served as our door and saw Mandor pacing up and down.

"Get up," he called, waving his arms. "I've

found out where I can get a philosopher's stone."

"Where?" Gus asked, a little crossly. Gus likes to sleep late.

"In ancient Egypt, in the Temple of the Goddess Isis, the philosopher's stone rests on an altar in the Inner Chamber. I found the reference in one of my books. Now, all I have to do is use my magic cheese to send you and Jaq back to ancient Egypt, to the Temple of Isis, and you can bring back just a little piece of the philosopher's stone. A tiny piece will do. We'll all be rich!"

I am never absolutely enchanted when Mandor talks about time-travel, mostly because it's Gus and I who do the traveling while Mandor stays home, snug in his tower. However, I always like to oblige the old magician, and so does Gus. We went up to the tower, where Mandor gave each of us a crumb of the magic cheese—a tiny crumb indeed, since we didn't want to spend days in ancient Egypt. Mandor said his incantation, spun around three times, and stamped his foot. The tower started to shimmer and fade away, and just as it did I saw the cat sniffing at the cheese. Then the tower was gone and Gus and I were standing in a wide-pillared, stone-paved corridor. It was dark, except for some torches that glimmered high up on the pillars.

"Don't like this place," Gus complained in a whisper.

I didn't like it, either. It was spooky—all that long, empty darkness. We set out, slipping through the shadows, trying not to make the tiniest noise on the stone floor.

"Something moved back there," Gus said nervously.

I tried to peer through the gloom, only I couldn't see anything but shadows dancing on the floor. We hurried on, stopping now and then to listen for a following footstep that we could never quite hear, or to search for a pursuing shape that always disappeared just as we turned our heads. I don't mind telling you, I was in a cold sweat. At last,

after what seemed like seven or eight years of trudging along the passageway, we came through a great door into a wide, brilliantly decorated room.

It was without windows, but it glowed with hundreds of torches. And raised up on a marble platform in the center of the room was a stone, and around the stone a group of young ladies, dressed in what appeared to be white nightgowns, were dancing and chanting.

Gus and I popped out of sight behind a pillar and waited until the young ladies had finished their dance and trooped out. Then we got a good look at the stone.

It was the philosopher's stone! It just had to be. It was beautiful—gold and green, flecked with amber and blue and white. If someone had asked me to imagine a stone that could change lead to gold, that's exactly how I'd have pictured it.

It only took us a moment to scramble up onto the platform. Mandor had said that just a tiny piece of the stone would do, and that's all we intended to take. We leveled off a chip, using a stout toy chisel and hammer which Mandor had provided for the expedition, and I put the stone chip in my pocket.

Suddenly I became aware that we were not alone! Watching us over the edge of the platform was a cat—a black, nasty, hungry-looking, cat-type cat!

I opened my mouth to squeak a warning to Gus. Too late! The cat was over the edge of the pedestal and had Gus's tail under his paw. I couldn't watch, yet I couldn't look away. It was horrible!

Just then there was a loud noise, as if a thousand tea kettles had started to boil at once. A black and white and gray and yellow *something* streaked into my line of vision, hissing and spitting, and landed with a bump on the pedestal. It was our cat—our very own cat!

For a moment he just glared at the black temple cat. Then he said something under his breath in cat language. It must have been something pretty bad, because the temple cat let go of Gus and glared back.

Our cat just stared at him. It was the strangest thing. I may have mentioned that our cat had a very odd way of looking as if he could read your mind. Well, conversation between the two cats would seem to indicate that some pretty fancy mind reading went on just then. No doubt our cat reminded the temple cat who it was that dug up the dahlia beds last week, not to mention who stole the fish from the temple kitchen, and who had been sneaking out in the evening to explore the garbage pails over at the Palace of the Pharaohs. The temple cat tried to hold his own, like a bad witness who is being cross-examined by a good district attorney, but he finally had to give in. He put his tail

between his legs and crept away, leaving Gus and me free and unharmed. And our cat accomplished the entire thing without ever raising a paw—by sheer mental power alone.

I was completely awed.

Needless to say, Gus and I lost no time in getting out of there. And needless to say, we took the great, the wonderful, the courageous, brave cat with us.

Mandor was overjoyed when we reappeared in his tower, complete with philosopher's stone and cat. As we had already guessed, the cat had tasted the cheese just as we had, and had been catapulted back to ancient Egypt with us—thank goodness!

We left Mandor happily melting lead in a saucepan he'd borrowed from the cook. He was getting all ready to make quantities of gold. We had more important things to do. For instance, we had to get our admirable cat a huge bowl of cream.

The Invisible Menace

Mandor the magician is the end—the living end. For years he's gone along as a complete failure. His love potions make people hate each other. His ulcer cures give folks the stomach ache. His wart removers will remove everything but warts. He can't even forecast the weather. So you could have knocked Gus and me over with the well-known feather when he actually proved himself as an alchemist.

As I've explained, Mandor used the magic cheese to send Gus and me back to ancient Egypt to get a piece of the philosopher's stone. This stone, carefully guarded and kept on an altar in an old temple, makes it possible to change lead into gold—provided you've got the right formula. Mandor claimed he had the formula, and we got him the stone. He was all set, and he went to work. "I'll make my mark as an alchemist," he kept muttering when we left him in his tower.

Lo and behold if we didn't go up the next morning to find Mandor, even shaggier than usual, with a large burn in the front of his best robe, surrounded by gold!

"I've done it!" he chortled when he saw us. "I've made gold! I'm a success at last!" And he did a sort of shuffling little jig.

Gus touched a piece of gold in a dazed sort of way and asked what I thought was a sensible question. "What you gonna' do with it, Mandor?"

"Do with it?" Mandor crowed. "Do with it? Why I'll . . . I'll . . . "

He stopped and looked confused. Obviously he hadn't thought that far ahead.

I suppose, when you come right down to it, Mandor didn't really want to be rich. He'd always had everything he needed at Cinderella's palace—a good home, steady job, plenty to eat, lots of time to putter, and nobody to bother him very much. Gus's question caught him short; he didn't know *what* he was going to do with the gold.

"I'll buy a new robe," he finally announced.

"Then what?" I asked.

"Why then I'll . . . I'll . . . "

He was still pondering when we heard a loud scream from the courtyard below. We rushed to the window and looked out in time to see the Captain of the King's Guard stagger around in a circle and fall to the ground in a dead faint.

"Shades of Zebulon!" Mandor yelled. He snatched up Gus and me, popped us into his pocket, and ran downstairs, his bony old legs taking the steps two at a time. In the courtyard we found the Captain of the Guard just coming out of his faint.

"He's gone—disappeared!" the captain yelled, pointing at the drawbridge, which was down.

"Who's gone?" asked the Keeper of the Imperial Coffe Urn, who'd run out from the pantry.

"The postman!" said the captain. He pointed again at the drawbridge.

"Hmph!" snorted the cook. "So the postman went away. What's so exciting about that? The man's daft."

"But he didn't just go away," the captain explained. There were actually tears in his eyes. "He walked out of here across that drawbridge, the way he does every morning after he's delivered the mail to the Imperial Secretary. He nodded to me the way he always does, and then he walked across the drawbridge and disappeared. Just on the other side of the moat, he vanished into thin air. It was as if he'd been swallowed up by some . . . some . . . SOMETHING!"

With that the brave Captain of the Guard forgot that he was the winner of the bronze oak leaf for courage in battle. He began to cry.

A fuzz-faced young second lieutenant was about to lead the captain away to the palace infirmary, convinced that the man had popped his top, when we saw the milkmaid from the nearby farm coming up the road. She was coming to deliver milk to the palace

kitchen. For some reason everyone in the courtyard stopped and watched her approach. We could see her clearly. That is, we could see her until she got within about three feet of the moat. She put her foot out to take a step and the foot vanished as if it had been cut off! Without noticing that she seemed to be minus one foot, she took her step and slid into nothingness. It was like watching a person walk through a door into another room, except that there wasn't any door and there wasn't any other room. There wasn't anything except a drawbridge, a moat, and an empty road.

Betsinda the chambermaid screamed. The cook went pale. The Keeper of the Imperial Coffee Urn said "Hmm-Ha!" and pulled at his moustache.

"Disappeared!" muttered the captain. "Just like the postman."

The second lieutenant, with a wild sort of look in his eye, drew his saber and charged

at the drawbridge yelling, "Villains! Stand and fight!"

He got across the drawbridge all right, but the minute he set foot on the other side he, too, vanished. *Pouff!* Cut off in mid-charge.

The days that followed took on a nightmare quality. Needless to say, no one tried to leave the castle via the drawbridge. The second assistant dishwasher in the imperial kitchen did slip out through a small gate in the north wall. He, too, disappeared completely in the twinkling of an eye, giving a case of hysterics to the scullery maid who'd been watching. So we knew that the "Zone of Disappearance," as the Court Chamberlain called it, extended all the way around the palace.

The King posted a guard on the parapets to warn travelers and townspeople away. And believe me, after the disappearance of the postman and the milkmaid, they didn't need much warning. No one—but no one—came near the palace. We were cut off—besieged as if an army had been camped around us.

With food enough on hand for a week,

we weren't too uncomfortable. But after the third day everyone grew very nervous. The cook snapped at the butler. The butler boxed the footman's ears. The footman had a spat with the upstairs maid, who, in turn, pinched the poor parlormaid severely.

It was on this third day that everyone remembered Mandor. No one understood the strange thing that had happened; wasn't it logical to ask the Official Court Magician to deal with it? The Chamberlain was the first to approach Mandor to see if, in some of the old books of magic lore, there might be a key to the secret that seemed to threaten the palace. The Chamberlain was almost immediately followed by the Lord Chancellor of the Privy Seal, and after the Lord Chancellor came the Keeper of the Royal Bedchamber.

Poor Mandor! He didn't know any more about what was going on than anyone else. I'll say this for him, though—he put up a good front. He took to looking wise—or at least as wise as Mandor can ever look, which isn't very—and he muttered things like, "It takes time," and "I'm on the trail of a very potent spell." His visitors would go away trying to be patient. There wasn't much else they could do.

It was our cat—our wonderful loyal vegetarian cat—who discovered that someone was patrolling the "Zone of Invisibility." The cat came to us on the evening of the third day and squeaked. (I mentioned, didn't I, that the cat never mewed? He squeaked. He thought he was a mouse, you see.) It was plain that he wanted to show us something. We followed him out across the courtyard and up to the drawbridge. There we stopped. But the cat went on and on until he'd almost crossed the bridge and we were sure we'd see *him* vanish any second, like the postman and the milkmaid. But not our cat. He was too smart! He stopped at the far end of the bridge and looked at the road and squeaked again. Then we saw what he saw. Footprints!

I don't mean old, dead footprints just lying there—footprints that might have been made by someone passing that way last week. These were brand new footprints. As a matter of fact, they were being made right there before us. We saw, one after another, the imprints of feet pressed into the dust of the road. And we heard clearly the tread of unseen feet. An invisible person was walking around the palace!

We took our news to Mandor. He wasn't much help. He only became more confused

61

trying to decide whether it was an invisible postman or an invisible milkmaid who was picketing the drawbridge.

Again, the cat helped us find the answer. He wandered into the kitchen and fell into an enormous canister of flour. He came howling and scurrying into the pink throne room, white as a ghost from the flour.

"He looks funny," Gus commented as the cat started to clean himself.

He did look funny. You'd never have been able to tell he was a black and gray and white and orange cat. He looked like a ghost of a cat.

With me, to think is to act. Within half an hour I'd mobilized all the mouse reserves in the palace. Every able-bodied mouse was called to an emergency meeting in the east ballroom. Speaking rapidly, I outlined my plan to them and, clearheaded mice that they are, they saw the logic of my idea immediately. Soon every mouse was armed with a small paper sack filled with flour. The cook protested, but Mandor threatened to cast a spell on her and she kept quiet after that.

Out we marched through the huge double portals of the palace. It was a thrilling sight!

A ghost!

It was then that I got one of my most outstanding ideas. I know that my career has been practically studded with outstanding ideas, but even for me, this one was a gem. Suppose we sprinkled our invisible pacer with flour. Wouldn't it stick to him, just the way it had stuck to our cat, and make him visible to us?

Hundreds of brave mice, each with a mission. We crossed the courtyard, then marched over the drawbridge to the very edge of the moat. Above us, high on the parapets, Mandor watched.

We stopped short of the "Zone of Invisibility," and we waited. But not for long. Soon we heard footsteps approaching. Then we saw them planting themselves on the ground,

one after another. A rose bush on the edge of the moat stirred, though there was no wind. The invisible one was there!

I shouted "Go!" and every mouse hurled his sack of flour into the air about five feet above the ground. The sacks burst; there was an immense billowing white cloud. Then the flour settled and we saw him!

The invisible one was a man—but what a strange man! He wore a weird flowing robe and had a crown on his head, the like of which I'd never seen. In his hand was a long staff. As the flour cleared, he realized what had happened. He saw us and pointed with his staff.

We did not hesitate upon the order of our going. We went! Helter skelter, we swarmed into the palace. But we'd accomplished our mission. We knew what the invisible menace looked like!

In Mandor's tower, we found the old magician shaking like a leaf.

"You see him, Mandor?" Gus asked.

Mandor groaned. "He's a priest of ancient Egypt—one of those who were keepers of the Temple of Isis, where the philosopher's stone rested."

Mandor groaned again. "I know why he's here. He's come across the years to get back that piece of the philosopher's stone we have. There must be some magical condition we don't understand that keeps him from entering the palace and taking the stone, but it also keeps us from leaving. Oh, what will I do? I've brought this terrible curse down on everyone here!" And the poor old soul began to weep.

"Give him back the stone," I suggested. Even Mandor should have been able to figure this out.

Mandor agreed. "That's what I'll have to do, before anyone else disappears. It was nice to be able to make gold. There isn't another magician alive today who can do it. But I'll give back the stone."

"Never mind, Mandor," I comforted him. "You can make yourself famous even without the gold."

"How's that?" Mandor asked.

"Don't tell anyone you've got a piece of the old Egyptian stone. Just say you've got the answer to the invisible menace, which is true. Then go out there tomorrow morning in front of the whole court and leave the stone on the other end of the drawbridge. The Egyptian will go back to Egypt and we'll go back to living normally. You've got it made."

So, early the next morning, Mandor put on his best robe, draped it carefully to hide the burned place, and marched across the drawbridge with the philosopher's stone in a little golden box. The entire court, watching from the parapets, saw him put the box on the drawbridge, but only Gus and I saw the lid of the box open, then close. Then the box slipped into invisibility.

Suddenly it began to rain people. First the postman dropped out of thin air onto the palace lawn. Then the milkmaid, the second lieutenant, and finally the dishwasher. None of them was hurt, but none could tell anything about where they'd been for three days.

That was the end of the invisible menace. From that day forward anyone could go or come freely. I'm sorry to say that Mandor's magic gold disappeared. In its place was just so much plain old lead. But Mandor didn't really care. He'd never wanted to be rich; he'd wanted fame and prestige. And now he had them, because everyone thought he'd been able to drive the menace away by his great magic. Mandor was smart enough never to tell anyone the truth about the whole affair. And, until now, so were Gus and I.

The Story of Timothy's House

This is the story of the house of Timothy Mouse, just as he told it to Dumbo. Dumbo was the little circus elephant with the very big ears, and Timothy was his best friend.

Timothy told Dumbo all about it one rainy afternoon when the circus show was over and little Dumbo, with his clown clothes on, was waiting for the second performance.

Timothy had traveled from town to town with the circus as long as he could remember. And as long as he could remember, Timothy had wanted a little private place in the circus that he could call his own.

It was all very well digging his way into a nice warm spot inside one of the bales of hay they always carried around for the elephants, but it was rather tiresome having to pick out a different bale each night. He even had a couple of narrow escapes when an elephant unexpectedly made up his mind to lie down on the hay.

Added to that, Timothy sometimes got hay fever. And a little mouse just doesn't dare sneeze at the wrong time. So Timothy wanted a regular home, a safe home, a home of his own.

"I stumbled on the idea of building a house," Timothy told Dumbo, "when I fell over an empty cheese carton outside the clowns' tent, in the dark."

The clowns had been eating cheese and crackers before they went to bed, and Timothy went to see what was left of the feast. The cheese was gone, but the container was there. It had a peaked roof and it *looked* like a house. Timothy put it on the framework under the floor of the ringmaster's car, right by a knothole so he could pop in and out easily.

That was a fine beginning, but of course Timothy needed a great many things to make it homelike.

First, he fixed up the outside. Naturally, he needed a chimney. So he hunted and he hunted and he hunted—and finally he found an old corncob pipe.

Then he found a thimble. He didn't know exactly how he could use it, but he knew it would come in very handy. So he took it with him.

And on his way home he saw a broken necklace of orange beads, so he brought that, too.

And still he needed a thing or two. He hunted and he hunted and he hunted—and finally he found a walnut shell and two gold-headed hatpins . . . some feathers from an old feather boa . . . and a cork . . . and a big clothespin. And he took them all.

On his way home he saw a broken necklace of blue beads, so he brought that too.

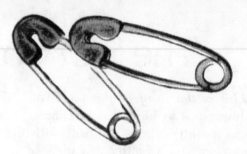

They didn't look like much, all lying in a heap, but Timothy went to work because, more than anything else, he wanted his own home.

And after a while he had everything in place—and he stood off and looked at it and he beamed with delight and threw out his arms and cried, "It's a mansion!"

BUT IT WAS EMPTY INSIDE!

So Timothy started out again. And he hunted and he hunted and he hunted and he found just what he wanted! A half-opened sardine can. So he took that.

And on his way home he saw a fat hairpin . . . and another cork.

The cork and the hairpin were easy to carry home, but the sardine can was heavy for just a little mouse. Then a boy came along, saw the can, and kicked it as he walked. His last kick sent it into a clump of grass not five feet from Timothy's home, and Timothy pulled it the rest of the way.

But his house wasn't half furnished yet, and off Timothy went again. And he hunted. And this time he found an overturned wastebasket. It had lots of very important things in it. There were safety pins . . . and a bottle top . . . and a piece of broken comb . . . and a collar button . . . and a beautiful postage stamp. And Timothy took them all.

He hurried back to the wastebasket and found what was left of a sock with broad red stripes.

He found more hairpins—they were *very* useful—and a bright gold button, which he polished until it shone.

And on his way home he found an old, cracked safety-razor blade. So he picked that up very carefully and took it home, too.

Now he really had a great deal to work with. So Timothy began to make things for the inside of his house. First he made a rocking chair. He used two safety pins, a cork, and the big hairpin.

Then he made a table out of two smaller hairpins and the bottle top. But best of all, so far, was his fireplace. There, right in the center of the side wall, was the sardine can with its lid rolled back to frame a hearth, and the piece of comb just fitting the front as a perfect fender.

Beside the fireplace was a bit of shingle with the razor blade handy to chop it up for firewood. The walnut shell was a wood basket. On the wall Timothy pasted the beautiful postage stamp which, with the golden button to balance it on the other side, made as fine a decoration as you can imagine. The old sock became a beautiful rug.

"There," said Timothy, "is a very fine living room for a mouse."

Next morning, Timothy made a rare find —a big stickpin! With an almost-real diamond in it!

"What could be better," cried Timothy, "as a mirror for my bathroom!" But then he remembered that he didn't have a bathroom. "Dear me," he said to himself.

So he hunted and he hunted and he hunted and finally he saw an old paper cup with a drinking straw beside it. And on his way home he found a playing card. Then he saw a half-empty packet of paper matches. He propped open the lid—and there he had a fine washstand. He stuck his almost-real diamond stickpin above it for a mirror. Then

he put the playing card on the floor for a mat.

And so he added to his home. Another pipe, with a lid, gave him a nice stove, and a key served as a poker.

Timothy loved music, too, so he made himself some lovely musical instruments. Some assorted pins, stuck through the side of a box lid and supported by a spool, gave him a zither to play.

He had a harp, too, made from more pins in a cork with a safety pin as a frame. (This was mostly for looks, because Timothy could never get much music out of it—it just added a good deal of elegance to the corner of his living room.)

But Timothy's prize possession was his chest for cheeses. This was a small candy box which still had its lacy paper frills around the edges. Partitions ran across it, and when Timothy stood it on end and filled it with bits of his favorite cheeses, carefully arranged to give the most delightful combinations of fragrant odors, it was, Timothy felt, the most wonderful thing of all.

Timothy's house was nearly complete. He made clothestrees by notching matches and standing them up straight. He picked some dandelions and put them in the thimble. It made a lovely vase.

But when night came and Timothy was very tired from all his work, he couldn't get a good rest. He didn't have a good bed. It was a nice springy scrubbing brush, with four old pencils for posts. But it had no mattress and no covers.

The rest of his bedroom was fine, Timothy thought. A matchbox was a bureau, and he had found a broken mirror for it. He had a chair, a rug—made of someone's lost handkerchief—and a beautiful cigar band for a wall decoration.

After a rather uncomfortable night, he decided that he *must* find some way to improve his bed. He hunted and he hunted and he hunted, but he could find nothing that was just right. He *did* find two more matchboxes, some buttons, and a bright penny. He made a table, with a drawer, from one matchbox. The other became a cabinet on one side of the living room. It contained his fine collection of buttons, the prize one of which Timothy had daringly gnawed off the best uniform of the ringmaster himself.

But he did not forget his bed. In the afternoon he did not go to the circus performance because he was so busy hunting. Finally he found it! A big, soft pocketbook with a plush lining!

Home he brought it, tugging it through the front door past its two pin pillars, past the sardine-box fireplace and his safety-pin rocking chair, through the bathroom with its paper-cup shower and the beautiful, almost-real diamond mirror, into his bedroom and up on top of the springy scrubbing brush.

"There," said Timothy, "is a royal bed for a mouse!"

And he climbed right in.

But somehow he couldn't get comfortable. First he tried to sleep on his right side. Then he tried to sleep on his left side. Then he tried to sleep on his back. And that was worst of all.

And then suddenly he had an idea. He sprang out of bed. He ran into the living room. He seized—very carefully—his razor-blade hatchet. And he rushed back to his pocketbook bed.

One—two! And there was a little hole right through the top side of the pocketbook.

Three—four! And there was his hat hanging on the post at the head of his bed.

Five—six! And there was Timothy himself back inside his bed.

Seven—eight! And there—look!—*there was his tail*, at last comfortable, sticking out through the hole in the pocketbook!

Nine—ten! And there was—ho-hum—oh, dear me, excuse me—there was—hmm—eh? What was that? Oh! Yes—Timothy—hum—There was Timothy Mouse sound asleep in his own bed in his own house. Ho—hum!

GOOD NIGHT!

Lambert the Sheepish Lion

Afterward, the sheep all said that the whole thing would not have happened except for Mr. Stork. The stork wouldn't admit that. Not for a second. It was the dispatcher's fault, said Mr. Stork. The dispatcher had wrapped the bundle. The dispatcher had addressed the label to the flock of sheep that lived in Tully's meadow.

The address couldn't be plainer. And underneath, to make sure there would be no mistake, the dispatcher had written, "Baby lambs. Handle with care."

Of course Mr. Stork *did* handle them with care. He hadn't been delivering babies for years and years without learning a thing or two or three. Even when he was caught in a strong down-draft on the way to the meadow, he never jostled his precious bundle.

Mr. Stork had started out at sunset. He liked to make his deliveries during the night. The full moon had risen by the time he circled above the meadow where the sheep were at pasture. He tilted his great wings this way and that way and floated down through the trees.

Mr. Stork put his bundle down on the ground and began to unwrap it. "Kind of a bumpy trip," said he, to anyone who might care to listen.

No one answered. In the meadow all around Mr. Stork, the mother sheep waited eagerly. Not one of them stirred as the stork finished unwrapping the bundle.

"Well, here we are now," said he.

The mother sheep smiled. One, two, three, four, five little lambs lifted their heads, opened their sleepy eyes and looked around.

"Up you get!" ordered Mr. Stork. "Now don't crowd. Just pick out the ewe that you like best, and she'll be your mother."

One, two, three, four, five little lambs got to their feet. They wobbled as they began to walk. But after a few steps they were more steady. In a moment or two five little lambs were snuggling up to five happy mother sheep.

But, "Oh, dear me!" said Mr. Stork. "Oh me, oh my!"

For the stork saw a sixth sheep. And he saw that she had no little lamb. She stood to one side and watched the ewes caress their new babies, and she looked as lonely as lonely can be.

"What could have happened?" wondered the stork. "I was sure I had enough to go around."

He picked up the bundle and shook it, hoping as hard as a stork can hope that there would be a baby lamb left in the bottom.

Sure enough, out tumbled a soft little ball of fluff!

"Why, you lazy little lamb!" exclaimed Mr. Stork. "Come on! It's time you were awake!"

The cuddly little thing unrolled itself. A

"Goodness!" exclaimed Mr. Stork. "That's not a lamb. That's not a lamb at all!"

Mr. Stork looked at the label on the bundle. Sure enough, it was addressed to the flock of sheep. So that was no help.

Next Mr. Stork took off his spectacles and polished them. Then he took out his order book. "There has to be some mistake," said he, and he turned the pages, reading orders for baby leopards and young lizards, tiny lynxes and infant llamas and little lambs.

"Aha!" said he at last. "That's it! You must be Lambert! And you're a lion. You don't belong here at all!"

Mr. Stork looked up from his order book. "Lambert?" said he.

pair of pale green eyes looked up at Mr. Stork. A rough pink tongue licked at a shiny black nose. A mouth opened wide in a yawn and Mr. Stork saw little needle-sharp teeth.

But Lambert the baby lion wasn't there. He had made his way to the lonely mother sheep and had nestled up to her, just as the little lambs had nestled up to the ewes they

had chosen to be their mothers. The lonely mother sheep was nuzzling Lambert, and she didn't look at all lonely any more. In fact, she looked like a very happy mother sheep.

Mr. Stork took out a pencil and made a notation in his order book. "Lambert," said he to himself. "Lion. South Africa. My stars! I have to do some flying!"

He put away the pencil and tucked the order book back into his vest pocket.

"Come, Lambert," he called.

Lambert paid not the slightest attention. He pressed closer to the mother sheep and purred.

Mr. Stork strode up to the sheep. "I'm very sorry that we've had a slight mix-up, Mrs. Sheep," he said, tipping his cap. "No need for you to worry about this vicious little brute.

I'll just take him away and drop him in the jungle, where he belongs." With that, the stork tried to pick Lambert up.

The next thing Mr. Stork knew, the mother sheep had butted him right straight up into the air. She had found a baby, and she did not intend to let him go again. And if he didn't look like every other little lamb in the pasture, she thought he was all the dearer for that!

Mr. Stork rubbed his damaged tail feathers. "Heavens to Betsy!" said he.

Mrs. Sheep lowered her head as if she might butt Mr. Stork again. As for Lambert, he opened his little mouth and showed his sharp little teeth.

"Well, all right!" exclaimed Mr. Stork. "You can have him. You can have anything you want. After all, I'm only a delivery service!"

And he flew back to headquarters, no doubt intending to have a word or two with the dispatcher who had made up his bundle.

As for Lambert, he snuggled down to sleep next to Mrs. Sheep. And when morning came and all the little lambs were being tidied up by their mothers, Lambert stood patiently while Mrs. Sheep smoothed down his little dark mane and fluffed out his tail. When Lambert was as neat and handsome as she could make him, Mrs. Sheep nudged him toward the little lambs.

And weren't those little lambs having a good time! Lambert scampered up to them with his rough little pink tongue hanging out. He was all ready to jump and gambol the way they did.

"Baaa!" The little lambs bleated a welcome to Lambert. "Baa. Baa."

Lambert tried to say "Baa." But when he opened his mouth, all that came out was a small "Meow!"

The little lambs had never heard such a thing. They tried bleating again, and again Lambert meowed.

The little lambs began to laugh. They laughed and laughed. And they leaped into the air, for little lambs love to leap. And they butted each other with their hard little heads, for little lambs love to butt.

At last, the little lambs began to sing a rather nasty song—the way small folk the world over sing when they want to make fun of someone who is different.

"*Lambert!*" sang the little lambs.
"*Lambert! Lambert!*
You can't even baa and you can't even bleat.
Your ears are too big, and so are your feet.
Your tail is too short, and so is your wool.
There isn't enough for one bag full!"

Lambert felt simply dreadful. At first he crept back to his mother to be comforted.

It was true. It was too true. Lambert's feet *were* too big. And his wool *was* too short. Strictly speaking, he didn't have wool at all. He was a very strange lamb indeed.

Lambert's mother fluffed up his fur and smoothed down his mane, and Lambert began to feel better. That's when he decided that he might be a strange-looking little thing, for a lamb, but that he would do the very best he could to act properly, the way a lamb should act.

So Lambert practiced gamboling and leaping—even though he fell over his own big feet.

Lambert practiced butting heads with the little lambs—even though he kept getting knocked silly when he collided with the hard, hard heads of the little lambs.

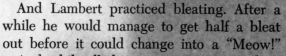

And Lambert practiced bleating. After a while he would manage to get half a bleat out before it could change into a "Meow!"

And while all this was going on, Lambert grew and grew and grew and GREW.

Lambert's mother was very proud of him. No one in the flock had ever had such a big lamb.

But Lambert wasn't proud. Deep down in his heart he knew that he was good for nothing.

He couldn't leap and he couldn't bleat.

He couldn't gambol and he couldn't butt.

He couldn't do a single earthly thing, except hide behind his mother when the lambs teased him too badly.

And after he got very large, he couldn't even hide very well.

In short, Lambert was a strange, yellow, cowardly, sheepish lion, and not a wild and woolly sheep.

Time passed. Spring became summer and summer became autumn. The little lambs were grown now. They really weren't little lambs any more. They were practically sheep.

But they were still young and they still liked to gambol and butt, and they still made fun of Lambert and played jokes on him and sang about him.

Lambert kept right on being a good sport about it but he *was* getting tired of it. He was tired of being butted into the pond every

time he bent over to take a drink. He was
tired of grinning his sheepish grin whenever
his playmates sang their nasty little song.
Most of all, he was tired of being different.

Then, one night when all the sheep were
fast asleep in the meadow, Lambert awoke
in a terrible fright. He had heard an awful
sound. He had heard a wolf howling in the
forest just beyond the meadow.

Lambert raised his head and pricked up
his ears and listened as hard as he could listen.

There it was again! And now Lambert could
see the wolf. The lean, hungry animal came
slinking out of the shadows. Its cruel yellow
eyes glinted in the moonlight. It drew back
its lips and Lambert could see horrid fangs.

A killer had found the flock!

Lambert was petrified. He hadn't the faint-
est idea what to do. He trembled and pressed
himself close to his mother. He hoped the
wolf wouldn't notice him.

Nearer and nearer came the wolf. Lambert

saw that the terrible beast was passing by
some of the sleeping sheep. It was headed
straight for him!

Lambert cowered behind his mother. The
wolf had come for him; there was no doubt
of it. He closed his eyes in terror.

Suddenly there was a scramble and a strug-
gle next to Lambert.

"Lambert!" The cry echoed in the night.

Lambert opened his eyes and looked
around. The wolf had seized his mother by
the leg and was pulling her away from the
flock toward the darkness of the forest.

"Lambert!" she bleated.

Now every ram and ewe in the flock was
awake. The lively ones who were so quick
to butt at Lambert were quite different now
that a hungry wolf was on the scene. With
a clatter of their sharp feet and a flit of their

white tails, they jumped to hide behind rocks and trees.

"Lambert!" called Lambert's mother. The wolf had her almost to the edge of the forest now. In a moment she would be gone forever.

With a desperate kick, Lambert's mother managed to free herself from the wolf. Still the hungry beast stood between her and the safety of the flock. He advanced on her slowly,

step by step. Without pity, he drove her back. Now she was not retreating toward the forest. She was going toward the edge of the cliff. Behind her was a straight drop of hundreds and hundreds of feet.

"Lambert!" she cried. At the very edge of the cliff, she stopped.

It was too much. At the sight of his mother crouching in terror before the wolf, something

GRR

snapped inside of Lambert. He forgot that he was a poor, miserable, cowardly, sheepish creature. In a twinkling, he became a raging lion.

Every hair in Lambert's huge, dark mane bristled and stood upright.

Lambert took a great breath. His enormous chest swelled.

The wolf had never before seen anything like Lambert.

Moreover, the wolf never wanted to hear or see anything like Lambert again. With a whimper, the wolf leaped over Lambert's mother and tried to hide.

Lambert was no sheepish coward now. He was a jungle monarch. He stepped past his

Then he opened his mouth and he roared a mighty roar. It was a roar that would have made the most ferocious lion in Africa proud.

Having announced his intentions in this way, Lambert unsheathed his huge claws and sprang at the wolf.

The wolf had never before heard anything like Lambert.

mother and quietly butted the wolf off the cliff.

The rams and the ewes came out from their hiding places one by one. After a moment or two, Lambert's mother stopped trembling. She was so proud of Lambert that she didn't quite know what to do.

What a celebration the sheep had then!

How glad they were that Lambert was one of them. They made up a brand new song that very moment, and they hoisted Lambert onto their shoulders and carried him around the meadow singing:

> *"Lambert, the sheepish lion,*
> *Lambert, there's no denying*
> *Now he's a wild and woolly sheep*
> *Instead of a sheepish,*
> *Wailing and weepish,*
> *Little Bo-Peepish lion!"*

So Lambert became the hero of the flock, and he and his mother lived happily ever after.

As for the wolf—well, he was lucky too, after a fashion. He didn't fall straight to the bottom of the cliff. He managed to catch hold of a bush that grew out of a narrow crevice half-way down. For all we know, he's there still. He may be quite hungry by now. But then, he won't starve. The bush has berries every spring!

84

The Golden Goose
A Funny Fairy Tale

Grandma Duck was a no-nonsense type of Duck. She ran her farm like a tight ship, so to speak, with no goofing off. The routine was simple: Up at 5:30, milk the cows, slop the pigs, weed the garden, feed the chickens, pasture the sheep, and THEN . . . breakfast!

Fethry Duck didn't realize what he was in for. He went to Grandma's for a week of relaxation away from smog, noise, hustle and bustle, and, above all, work. He was really dragging one day when Grandma Duck clapped an ax in one hand, a picnic basket in another, and told him to chop wood for the stove.

"You've gotta be kidding, Grandma," said Fethry, nervously tugging at his turtleneck sweater. "I mean, already my blisters have blisters. Two swings with this ax, and my hands will dissolve."

"Stuff and nonsense, sonny," said Grandma. "A little exercise will firm up those shoulders."

"What shoulders?" asked Fethry. And he was right.

"Well, anyway, I need some wood. And *you're* elected," Grandma stated, and that was the end of the matter.

"Where do I chop this wood?" asked Fethry, resigned to the task ahead.

"At that close batch of trees over there," she answered, pointing somewhere toward the north.

So it was that Fethry set forth to chop wood. He walked along the north side of the east forty and the east side of the north forty, and over the ridge, down the valley and along the stream until he arrived, an hour and a half later, at "that close batch of trees over there."

By this time he was quite hungry, and he set out Grandma Duck's picnic lunch. He was about to take the first bite when a

funny little old man appeared. The little old man looked closely at Fethry and at Grandma Duck's spread of goodies, and he asked, "Will you share your food with me?"

"Why not?" said Fethry, for though he was a little scatterbrained, he had a good heart. The little old man sat down and proceeded to put away a goodly share of the sandwiches, cakes, pies, tarts, cheese, fresh fruit, and homemade apple cider.

When he had finished, he leaned back, patted his stomach, and said, "You were kind to share your meager lunch with me. You have a good heart, and you shall not go unrewarded."

Fethry was examining his blisters and studying the ax handle, so he wasn't really paying attention. But he did hear the little old man say, "If you will look under that gorse bush, you will find a reward."

Fethry looked under the bush, and there he found a goose with feathers of pure gold.

"This goose could be valuable," Fethry thought to himself. He turned to thank the little old man, but the man was gone. Thinking that Grandma Duck might be interested in this new type of goose, happy-go-lucky Fethry trotted off in the direction of the farm.

Fethry may have had a good heart, but he had a terrible sense of direction. First thing he knew, he was lost. He walked and walked, and eventually came to an inn. The sun was beginning to set, so Fethry figured he'd better spend the night at the hotel and continue the search for Grandma Duck's farm in the morning.

Now it so happened that Scrooge McDuck was also spending the night at this particular hostel. Scrooge, as everybody knows, is the world's richest Duck. What was he doing at this modest wayside inn? "I didn't keep all my money by staying at the Ritz, Charley," was the way Scrooge expressed it.

Scrooge was sitting in the lobby with his copy of the *Wall Street Journal*, when Fethry Duck entered. Scrooge sniffed and sniffed again. Gold! He could detect it anywhere.

He put down his newspaper and saw Fethry with the goose under his arm. Scrooge's eyeglasses popped clean off his nose.

A Golden Goose!

Scrooge longed to touch it!

But Scrooge was a gentleman, and he knew that proper people did not go up to strange geese and lay hands on the feathers. Scrooge, therefore, determined to wait until dark, when he could caress the golden plumage without being seen.

That night he crept into Fethry's room. The goose was sleeping on the floor, and Scrooge crawled forward and put his hands on the feathers. What a wonderful feeling! Pure gold.

Scrooge tried to pull his hands away, and couldn't! He was stuck fast to the goose. When Fethry awakened in the morning, he found the world's richest Duck unable to separate himself from the Golden Goose.

"Are you in the habit of stealing into other people's rooms in the middle of the night to touch their geese?" Fethry asked.

"Shut up and unglue me from this thing," Scrooge snapped.

"How?"

"Go and get Huey, Dewey, and Louie. They all belong to the Junior Woodchucks, and Junior Woodchucks know everything."

So Fethry bounced downstairs and found Huey, Dewey, and Louie. The three boys were building a color television camera from bits and pieces of old glass and aluminum soft drink containers. Fethry watched them a while, then asked, "How did you kids learn how to do that?"

Huey said, "Our Junior Woodchuck Guide. It tells how to do everything."

"Then you better take it upstairs to my bedroom. Your Uncle Scrooge has troubles."

Quickly the boys forgot about the camera and went to aid Uncle Scrooge. But alas, their Junior Woodchuck Guide contained nothing about parting rich uncles from Golden Geese.

So they wrapped their arms around Scrooge and tried to pull him loose. This was a bad idea. First, it didn't work; second, the neph-

ews found themselves stuck fast to Scrooge McDuck!

"We can spend the rest of our lives here in this hotel room," Scrooge complained. "So we'll have to go in search of a goldsmith or a chicken plucker or somebody with a chisel."

Fethry agreed, so they all trooped out of the inn and set off down the road. Soon they ran into Daisy Duck, who was out shopping.

They immediately pleaded with her to free them from the Golden Goose.

"It's easy," she said, and she tugged at Huey. But no sooner had she touched him than she also became attached to the Golden Goose.

As they continued their trek, they were spied by the Beagle Boys. For years the Beagles had been trying to steal Scrooge's

gold, here he was, in broad daylight, walking down the road with a Golden Goose. The temptation was too much for the Beagles—they rushed forward and grabbed the goose from Scrooge. But they, too, became stuck to the feathers. Frantically they tried to pull away, but to no avail.

By this time it was pretty difficult walking. Either the three Beagles or else Scrooge, Huey, Dewey, Louie, and Daisy had to walk backwards. Fethry, who owned the goose, couldn't get near it. He walked along the edge, herding them in the proper direction. And everybody was getting desperate.

Now it happened that their route took them by the Royal Palace. And in the palace lived a king and his daughter. The king was a happy soul, but the little girl refused to laugh. The king had tried everything to bring

a trace of a smile to her lips, but nothing worked.

The court jester brought a frown. The king of TV comics brought a scowl. And that pair of goonies who set five new records in Las Vegas—they brought a bored yawn.

The king was in despair. As he tried, for the thousandth time, to figure out what to do, he heard happy cries from the royal nursery. He rushed inside, and there was the princess, laughing her head off. The king looked out the window, and he saw the silly group of travelers which had brought such joy to his daughter.

Immediately he sent for Fethry Duck and his companions. When they were gathered in the Royal Throne Room (with the princess still giggling to herself), the king thanked them all.

"What can I do for you people who have brought such joy to my daughter?" he asked.

Before Fethry could answer, Scrooge McDuck spoke up. "Do you know anybody who can separate us from this idiotic Golden Goose?"

"Certainly. *I* can," replied the king. He waved his hand in the air, and immediately they all came loose, tumbling and falling over each other.

Scrooge was amazed. "How did you manage to do it?" he asked.

"I can do anything. How do you think I got to be king?"

"In that case," said Fethry, "you keep the Golden Goose. It wouldn't do me any good anyway—I'd only get stuck with it."

"Thank you," said the king.

"My pleasure," said Fethry.

The king then ordered the Beagle Boys

clamped into the Royal Jail, he promoted Huey and Dewey and Louie to Junior Woodchuck First Class, and he invited Daisy and Scrooge to stay for dinner. He invited Fethry, too, but Fethry said, "Sorry, king, old buddy, but I've got to get back to Grandma Duck's farm." And he left the castle.

He was back at the farm before nightfall, having been given detailed directions by the Royal Mapmaker. He walked into the farmhouse, and Grandma Duck was there to meet him. She had just finished re-roofing the barn and digging a new root cellar.

"Where's my wood?" she demanded.

"Now, Grandma," Fethry began. "It's like this—"

"Are you going to give me a cock-and-bull story about some little old man with a Golden Goose?" she said, stamping her foot.

"Why, yes, now that you mention it."

"You can just forget it, sonny. I've heard that one before. Now tomorrow morning, I want you to chop that wood, or nobody gets any dinner."

And next day, that's exactly what Fethry did.

Chicken Little
A Funny Fairy Tale

Chicken Little lived with her mother and father, Mr. and Mrs. Samuel J. Little, in a pink house at the edge of a large oak grove. She was kind of a dumb kid, and she was flunking math, geography, and science. She didn't do much but sit around and daydream.

This was OK with her mother and father. Mr. Little was away most of the day, spraying his oak trees, and Mrs. Little stayed in the house and tidied up. She cleaned out closets, cupboards, wine cellars, gardening sheds— anything that had a speck of dirt in it. So when Chicken Little chose to sit outside and dream the Big Dreams of Tomorrow, both her mother and father were glad to be left alone.

Chicken was sitting under an oak tree one day, dreaming about becoming a princess and wearing a crimson silk dress, when a tiny acorn fell on her head.

94

Now, if Chicken Little hadn't been flunking science, she would have known that acorns come from oak trees, and they fall off all the time. But she didn't know this, and instead she thought the sky was falling. She jumped up and said to herself, "Oh my, the sky is falling! I must go and tell the king!"

But first she went to her mother to get permission to see the king. Mrs. Little was busy cleaning out under the sink, and she had no time for her daughter. The little girl said, "Mother, Mother, the sky is falling! I must go and tell the king!"

Her mother said, "That's nice, dear. Be home in time for dinner." And so Chicken Little set off down the road.

If Chicken Little hadn't been flunking geography, she would have known that the road to the king's palace was to the left, under the freeway, and straight up the hill. But she didn't know this, so she ran down the path to the right, in the wrong direction.

KING'S PALACE
UNDER FREEWAY

She ran into the forest, and the first person she met was Donald Duck. Donald was out with his bow and arrow, trying to shoot some game for dinner. But he hadn't found anything. In fact, he had lost three arrows —and his temper. He was very angry.

He saw Chicken Little running toward him. "Hi, Chicken," he said. "Seen any moose or elk or anything I can shoot for dinner?"

"No time for that," she answered. "I'm in a big hurry."

"How come? Where are you going?"

"I'm going to tell the king the sky is falling."

"Sky falling?" gasped Donald. "No wonder I haven't been able to hit anything with my bow and arrow."

"Yes," said Chicken Little. "I bet the sky kept getting in the way."

"Obviously," Donald reasoned. He added, "How do you *know* the sky is falling? Tell me—are you *sure*?"

"I saw it with my eyes. I heard it with my ears. And a piece of it fell on my head."

"Well," said Donald, "I'll come with you and we'll tell the king together!" So they went running down the road.

Soon they came to Goofy. He was lying in a hammock, taking a snooze. He opened one sleep-filled eye and gazed at them. "Duh, what's up?" he asked.

"Not up. *Down*." Chicken Little said excitedly. "The sky is falling!"

Though Goofy is not noted as a great thinker, he did a little thinking. And looking. He stared upward at the sky. "It looks as far away as it usually does," he observed. "How do you know it's falling?"

"I saw it with my eyes. I heard it with my ears. And a piece of it fell on my head."

97

"Gol-lee, then you must be right. If I were you, I'd go and tell the king."

Donald Duck piped up, "That's exactly what we're going to do. Do you want to come with us?"

"I guess so. I was getting tired of sleeping anyway."

So Goofy got out of his hammock, and the three of them went off to tell the king.

They hurried through the woods, and soon they found Mickey Mouse sitting on a log reading a book. Now Mickey Mouse is a pretty smart cookie, and not one to fall for any lame-brain story about a falling sky.

"Hi there, Goof," he said to Goofy. "Where ya going?"

"To tell the sky the king is falling," said Goofy.

"No, Goofy," Donald Duck corrected him. "To tell the *king* the *sky* is falling."

"You've got to be kidding," said Mickey.

"No, Mick. Ask Chicken Little. She'll tell you."

Mickey asked her, "How do you know the sky is falling?"

Chicken answered, "I saw it with my eyes. I heard it with my ears. And a piece of it fell on my head."

Mickey was doubtful. "I haven't read anything about it in any of my books. In fact, I never heard of such a thing."

"Of course not," Donald explained. "This is the first time. This is something *new*."

Mickey still wasn't so sure they were right, but he thought it wouldn't hurt if he were to go along to see the king. So he joined in, and the four of them trotted off through the forest.

Soon they passed a little cottage. There, standing in the doorway, was Minnie Mouse. Before anybody could say anything, she spoke up. "Why, you're in time to help me with my cake."

"But we're in a hurry, Minnie," said Mickey, "the sky is falling and—"

"It can wait!"

"Wait for what?"

"For me to finish my cake," Minnie replied. "I'm about to mix everything together, and I need a few strong right arms."

Before they knew what had happened, Minnie had herded them together in the kitchen. "It's an extra big cake," she explained, "so I need to double the recipe."

And she set Donald to breaking eggs, Goofy to sifting flour, and Chicken Little to doubling the amount of baking powder. Unfortunately, Chicken Little was flunking math, and she mumbled to herself, "Let's see now. Two times three is . . . *ten!*" So she put ten teaspoons of baking powder in the batter.

When the cake was ready to go in the oven, Donald and Goofy and Mickey and Chicken Little said good-bye to Minnie.

Minnie was surprised that they weren't staying. "Where are you going in such a hurry?" she asked.

Chicken Little answered, "To tell the king the sky is falling."

Minnie was surprised. "How do you know the sky is falling?"

"I saw it with my eyes. I heard it with my ears. And a piece of it fell on my head."

"Oh, dear," said Minnie, "then maybe I'd better go along. I can use an oven at the palace and save on the gas bill." So she joined them, with her cake batter in a bowl which she carried under her arm.

They hadn't gone more than a quarter mile when they met the Big Bad Wolf. He was prowling through the bushes looking for the Three Little Pigs. When he saw Chicken

Little and Donald and Goofy and Mickey and Minnie with her cake batter, he forgot about the pigs.

Wiping the pine needles off his hat and putting on his best manners, he asked, "Why hello, you-all. Where are you going on this warm day?"

"To tell the king the sky is falling," said Chicken Little.

"The sky? Falling? Well, I declare. How can you tell?"

"I saw it with my eyes. I heard it with my ears. And a piece of it fell on my head."

"Yes, I can see that," murmured the sly old wolf. Brightening, he suggested, "Why don't you-all come to my house for a mint julep and a bit of refreshment?"

"But we've got to see the king," said Chicken Little.

"Ah, little one," cautioned the wolf, "the palace is a long way off, and if the sky falls right away, you'll need the protection of a sturdy roof."

"I guess you're right," Chicken Little agreed.

"Then let's go on over to my place," the wolf said, "and wait to see what happens."

So they did. Chicken Little, Donald Duck, Goofy, Mickey Mouse and Minnie—they all went to the Big Bad Wolf's shack in the woods.

No sooner had they entered the house than the Big Bad Wolf slammed the door shut and locked the heavy-duty padlock. Then he ran around to the window. "Why don't you put the cake in the oven to bake. I'll mosey down to the General Store for some candles, and we'll all have a dandy party."

Chicken Little clapped her hands in joy. "Oh, good! I like parties."

"Hmmmm. So do I," the wolf muttered to himself. He slammed the window shut and jogged down the lane to the store. He thought to himself, "My, what a fine dinner I'm going to have—chicken, duck, AND a cake. Oh, boy! My birthday isn't until August, but I think I'll celebrate tonight."

Minnie was very sad. "I don't know what could have happened to my cake. I measured everything so carefully." Alas, poor Minnie would never know that Chicken Little couldn't add. She had put enough baking powder in that cake to level the Taj Mahal.

In the excitement of the Big Bad Wolf's shack blowing up, they all forgot about the sky falling. Chicken Little ran home to her mother's clean house. Goofy ran back to his hammock. Mickey ran back to his book. And Minnie ran home to tear up that cake recipe.

He was far away when the sky darkened and BOOM! Minnie's cake blew up. The door of the house fell out, the windows fell in, and the roof sailed somewhere into the next county. Scrambling out came Chicken Little, Mickey Mouse, Minnie Mouse, Donald Duck and, last but not least, Goofy.

And it's just as well they never got to the palace, for the king wasn't there. He was out for the day, attending the royal ball game.

And the Big Bad Wolf? What of him? He came back and saw his house flat on the ground. And he held his face in his paws and wailed, "Oh, my! The sky *did* fall— right on top of my house!"

The Gingerbread Man
A Funny Fairy Tale

M innie Mouse was busy in her new air-conditioned, all-gas-and-electric, Green Ribbon kitchen. It had stainless steel counter tops, walnut-paneled walls, non-skid tile on the floor, non-glare glass in the windows, hidden fluorescent lighting, a teakwood spice cabinet, and a complete set of all the new uncrackable and unmeltable mixing bowls. Considering the equipment she had to work with, she could have cooked a gourmet dinner for any gourmet—even a king.

So what did she cook? A gingerbread man. A lone, solitary gingerbread man. It had two raisins for eyes, a cherry for a nose, and three currants for buttons down his front. As a matter of fact, it was a handsome gingerbread man, as gingerbread men go. And as gingerbread men go, this one went!

102

It happened after Minnie had set him to cool on the maple-grained plastic no-stain table top. One minute the gingerbread man was there, and the next he wasn't. He had pushed open the kitchen door and rushed out into the garden like a Notre Dame halfback. Minnie saw him running down the path.

She knew he wouldn't last long in the outside world, so she cried, "Stop! Stop!"

As he ran away, the Gingerbread Man sang:

"*Run run run,*
As fast as you can;
You can't catch me
I'm the Gingerbread Man."

Minnie put her hands on her hips and stamped her foot. "We'll see about *that*," she snorted. And she started after him.

Sprinting down the road, he came upon Mickey Mouse's nephews, Morty and Ferdie. Minnie called to them, "Help me save the Gingerbread Man." Morty and Ferdie were on their way to try out for the local football team, and they took the proper stance to tackle the Gingerbread Man.

But he speeded up, gave them a swivel hip, and scooted between them, running to daylight. As he ran away, he called:

"*Run run run,*
As fast as you can;
You can't catch me—
I'm the Gingerbread Man.
I ran away from Minnie
And I can get away from you."

Morty and Ferdie, the would-be linebackers, were humiliated. "Stop! Stop!" they yelled. But the Gingerbread Man didn't stop.

The Gingerbread Man ran farther down the road. Pretty soon he came to Chip 'n Dale. The two perky chipmunks were passing an acorn back and forth like a football, when the Gingerbread Man ran by.

"Hi, Gingerbread Man! Wanna run pass patterns?" asked Chip.

But the Gingerbread Man didn't. He sang:

> *"Run run run,*
> *As fast as you can;*
> *You can't catch me—*
> *I'm the Gingerbread Man.*
> *I got away from Minnie*
> *And those two scrub tacklers*
> *And I can get away from you."*

The chipmunks looked down the road and, sure enough, there were Minnie and Morty and Ferdie, all chasing the Gingerbread Man.

"Looks like fun," said Chip. So they joined in the game, whatever it was.

Soon they were running through the woods. Of course, they weren't the only ones running in the woods. The Three Little Pigs were running for their very lives. Behind them was the Big Bad Wolf. Practical Pig, who happened to be in the lead, shouted, "OK, guys, play number 21-53-B." At that moment his brothers slowed down enough to let the wolf grab their curly tails.

Then one pig ran on the right side of a big pine tree, and his brother ran on the left side. The Big Bad Wolf was too greedy to let go of either tail, so—

BONK!

He hit his head on the tree, and half a

dozen pine cones fell to the ground. He let
go of the pigs' tails and rubbed his head. He
tried to run again, but he slipped on the
fallen pine cones. This gave the pigs time to
run home to their little brick house and slam
the door and bolt it.

At that moment the Gingerbread Man ran
by their cottage. Practical opened the window
and yelled, "Hey, Gingerbread Man, you're
getting into wolf country. Come on in here.
We'll help you.'

The Gingerbread Man wasn't about to believe Practical, either. Instead, he shouted:

> "Run run run,
>   As fast as you can;
>   You can't catch me—
>   I'm the Gingerbread Man.
>   I got away from Minnie
>   And those two scrub tacklers
>   And those pint-sized acorn tossers
>   And I can get away from you."

107

Practical was astounded that anybody would doubt his sound advice. He yelled, "But you don't know about the Big Bad Wolf. He's tricky. Stop! Stop!"

The Gingerbread Man had heard the word "Stop" so many times that he knew only one thing—when anybody yells "Stop" all good gingerbread men should keep going!

The pigs stared at each other in astonishment. "We can't let him go any farther, or he's done for."

The other two pigs agreed, so they threw caution to the winds and took off after the Gingerbread Man.

The Gingerbread Man led them deeper and deeper into the woods, and soon he came to a river. Sitting at the edge of the river was the Big Bad Wolf. He was holding a damp cloth to his aching head when the group appeared on the trail. There was the Gingerbread Man, followed by Minnie, Morty, Ferdie, Chip 'n Dale, and the Three Little Pigs. At first the Big Bad Wolf didn't believe what he was seeing. "What's this?" he asked—"is everybody in these woods in training?"

By this time the Gingerbread Man was

getting tired. He thought the Big Bad Wolf looked like a kindly old codger, so he decided to seek his help.

"Kindly Old Codger," the Gingerbread Man said, "I must escape from those single-minded people. You appear to be a Nice Person, so would you please take me across the stream?"

"My pleasure," sneered the Wolf. "I am here to help—heh-heh-heh."

So the Gingerbread Man jumped on his back, and the Big Bad Wolf started swimming.

On the bank of the stream, everybody was very unhappy.

"We tried to warn him," said the Three Little Pigs.

"We were a fraction of a second too slow," complained Morty and Ferdie.

"Him make great split-end," said Chip.

Minnie was disgusted with the whole thing.

'Well, back to my Never-Fail kitchen stove, with the solid bronze casters," she said.

And they all turned sadly around and went home.

All except the Big Bad Wolf, who was swimming slowly across the stream. He was in no hurry.

Presently the Gingerbread Man said, "Mister, I am getting wet."

"Then jump on my head," said the Wolf.

After a while the Gingerbread Man said, "Mister, I am getting wet even on your head."

"Then jump on my nose," said the Wolf.

So the Gingerbread Man jumped on the Wolf's nose. Which was his last mistake.

Gobble. Crunch. Smack.

In a minute the Big Bad Wolf had eaten him up.

Which is what eventually happens to all gingerbread men.

Duck in Boots
A Funny Fairy Tale

Today everybody knows that Scrooge Mc-Duck is without doubt the world's richest duck. His vaults filled with gold, his swimming pool filled with money—these are common sights along the highway. His stinginess, his penny-pinching—these are common topics of conversation around the world.

But the McDuck family wasn't always rich. There was a time when Scrooge's great-great-great-grandfather was penniless. In fact, he had nothing to call his own except a nephew named Donald.

"Wak," said Donald one day. "We shall soon die of hunger, Uncle Scrooge, for I know of no way to earn a living."

Scrooge of old, much like Scrooge of today, did not give up easily. "No," he said, leaning on his cane, "I have an idea. Maybe not a good idea, but an idea. Get me a sack and a pair of boots."

Donald thought that hunger pangs were affecting Uncle Scrooge's brain. "Sack? Boots?" he muttered to himself. But he hunted in the attic until he found an old burlap sack and a splendid pair of shiny boots. He gave them to Scrooge, who set off into the woods. When he came to a clearing he put down the sack. (Fortunately for Scrooge the sack had some juicy carrots in it, otherwise the story would have ended right here.)

Soon a fat rabbit came by and sniffed the carrots. As the rabbit sniffed the carrots, Scrooge popped him into the sack and tied it up.

Then, whistling merrily, he walked down the road to King Mickey's palace. So important did he look in his shiny boots that the palace guards took him straight to the king. Scrooge bowed low.

"Sire, my master begs you to accept this small gift."

"And who is your master?" asked King Mickey, delighted at the plump rabbit.

"The Marquis of Carabas," said Scrooge, repeating a name he had heard once in a fairy tale.

Bowing low again, Scrooge went away.

After that he returned every day with a gift for King Mickey, who grew more and more impressed with the generosity of the so-called Marquis of Carabas.

"Sir Scrooge, you must bring me your kind master, for I long to meet him," said Mickey.

One day Scrooge learned that King Mickey was going on a journey with Princess Minnie. Scrooge ran home as fast as his boots would carry him.

111

"Quick, Donald! The king will be driving by in his carriage. Run to the river, take off your clothes, and jump in!"

"Why should I jump in the river?" asked Donald, quite reasonably.

"This is no time to ask silly questions," said Scrooge.

"Silly?" squawked Donald. "That river is cold."

"Never mind," Scrooge said, pushing Donald into the river. SPLASH!

"Glub, glub—wak . . . wak . . . WAK!!" yelled Donald.

At that moment King Mickey drove by in the royal carriage.

Scrooge ran toward the carriage, crying, "Help! My master, the Marquis of Carabas, is drowning. Some thieves stole his clothes and threw him in the river."

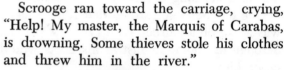

At once the carriage stopped, and Donald was pulled, dripping, from the river. Mickey, delighted to meet the Marquis at last, insisted on opening up the royal clothes trunk. Soon Donald, handsomely dressed in silks and satins, bowed before the king.

"Sir Marquis, allow me to drive you to your castle," said Mickey in his best King's English.

"I will run ahead and prepare the way," said Scrooge quickly, and he was off in a flash.

Scrooge came to some peasants named Huey, Dewey, and Louie working in a field.

"Tell the King that this land belongs to the Marquis of Carabas," said Scrooge. Huey, Dewey, and Louie giggled, but said they would obey.

113

Scrooge ran from field to field, telling all the workers the same thing.

At last he came to a huge castle, the home of Madam Mim. He knew she had power to work magic.

"Hi there, Mim," said Scrooge.

"Go away," said Madam Mim rudely. "I'm expecting visitors for dinner." She made a grab at Scrooge, but Scrooge skipped nimbly out of the way and thunked her, clump on the shin with his cane.

In a purple rage (her favorite color), Mim turned herself into a roaring lion.

Hanging by his cane from a chandelier, Scrooge said, "It is all right for you to turn yourself into a big lion. But I bet you eight million dollars you can't turn yourself into a tiny beetle! You are not clever enough for that!"

"Oh, yes I am," said Mim, and in a flash she became a tiny beetle—a ladybug, to be exact. Scrooge dropped to the floor, picked up a glass bottle, and popped the ladybug inside.

Madam Mim scratched in vain on the smooth glass trying to get out, but she could not. "Maybe in a few centuries, I'll let you loose," said Scrooge. "Your magic power should wear off by then!"

At that moment the royal carriage arrived. "Welcome to Carabas Castle," said Scrooge. "As you can see, a feast is prepared for you."

When King Mickey finished dinner, he said, "My dear Carabas, you have wonderful lands and a beautiful castle. And you serve the best roast pork this side of the Big Bad Wolf. It is a shame that you have all this, and your good friend Scrooge McDuck has nothing. Because he is such a good friend of yours, I hereby proclaim that Scrooge McDuck shall be named Lord McDuck with the best harvest lands in the kingdom."

"If you don't mind," said Scrooge, "I'd rather somebody else had the good harvest lands. I'll settle for those worthless, rocky mountains where nobody can till the soil."

King Mickey agreed. And that is how the Scrooge McDuck fortune got started. All it took was a sack of carrots and a pair of splendid boots—oh, yes, and a nimble brain to match the boots. (At least a brain nimble enough to know those untillable mountains contained mines rich in both silver and gold.) And if your brain is nimble, maybe you can do the same.

The Little Red Hen
A Funny Fairy Tale

*O*ne day the Little Red Hen went looking for treasure. She had heard about the miller's son who had found a sack of gold under a rock in the road. She had heard about the wise old man who gave the poor shepherd boy a golden goose. She had heard about the leprechauns with their bags of gold under thorn bushes.

So she decided to get some of this loot for herself. With her little wicker basket under her arm, she went forth. By the end of the day she was scratched from the thorns, tired of speaking to dull old men, and she had muscle strain from lifting rocks out of the road. And did she find any treasure? You bet she didn't.

On the way home, however, she did find a grain of wheat on the road. "Oh-ho," she cackled to herself. "This is an omen. I will plant it and reap it and grind it and bake it and have some bread for my tea. And somewhere along the line a handsome prince will come by and eat the bread and I'll move into the palace." At this stage of the game, she was willing to settle for head cook in the castle, in case the prince already had a princess.

So she picked up the grain of wheat and carried it home.

Next day, bright and early, she went to the field to plant the grain of wheat. On the way to the field she saw Gus Goose asleep under a spreading maple tree.

She went up to Gus and asked, "Will you help me plant this grain of wheat?"

"Not I." replied Gus, opening his eye barely enough to see whom he was talking to. "Sorry, Little Red Hen, but I've just returned from my vacation, and I'm resting up."

"Well, if that's the way you're going to be, I'll have to plant it by myself," she said. And she marched on toward the field.

Pretty soon she found Donald Duck, sitting cross-legged on the grass playing his bongo drums. *Trippity-thud-trippity-boom* went the bongos. Donald looked up. "Hi, Chickie-baby," he said.

The Little Red Hen decided he had her confused with Chicken Little (which indeed he had). She said, "Will you help me plant this grain of wheat?"

Trippity-thud-trippity-boom! "I don't plant seeds, I *eat* them," Donald replied.

The Little Red Hen knew the handsome prince would never come by if she didn't plant the seed, so she walked on toward the field. Pretty soon she found Donald Duck's three nephews, Huey and Dewey and Louie. They were sitting on the ground, close together. She approached them and said, "Will you help me plant this grain of wheat?"

"Shhhh," said Louie. "We're listening to the dragon fights on our transistor radio. No time for planting right now—the dragon is ahead of Saint George on points."

"Then I will plant it myself," she said. And she walked to the edge of the field. There she dug a small hole with her trowel, dropped in the seed, patted down the rich brown earth, and went away. She knew the hot sun and the warm rain would make her seed grow.

The seed did grow, and soon the time came for the Little Red Hen to reap the wheat.

On her way to the field she passed Gus Goose. He was still asleep. "Will you help me reap my wheat?" she asked.

"Sorry, Little Red Hen," Gus answered. "But it was a long hard vacation, and I haven't caught up on my resting yet."

"Then I will reap it myself," she said.

The Little Red Hen walked on, and soon she came to Donald Duck who was pounding on his bongo drums.

"Reaping time!" called the Little Red Hen.

"Great, Chickie!" said Donald. "I'd help you, but I have to finish my practice session."

Trippity-thud-trippity-boom went the bongos.

"If I wait for you to finish, I may never get my wheat reaped," said the Little Red Hen.

Nearing the field, she saw the three Duck nephews. Again they were grouped around their transistor. Deciding to try a different approach, she walked up smiling and said, "Oh, boy, am I going to have fun! I'm going to reap my wheat."

"Have your fun," said Dewey, looking up from the radio. "Saint George finally has the dragon on the ropes, and we couldn't leave now, even if we wanted to."

"Then I will reap it myself," she said as

she moved away. Arriving at the field, she took out her scythe and reaped the lone stalk of wheat.

Once she had reaped the wheat, she had to take it to the mill to be ground into flour. So she went to Gus Goose and asked, "Who will help me grind my wheat?" But Gus was resting up from his morning nap and didn't answer.

She went to Donald Duck and asked, "Who will help me grind my wheat?"

Donald closed his eyes and grinned. "Listen to this!" he said. And the bongo drums went *trippity-thud-trippity-boom.*

"If that's an answer, I'm sorry I asked," said the Little Red Hen.

Then again she heard the Duck nephews' transistor radio. "Who will help me grind my wheat?" she asked the boys.

"Not now," Huey said. "The dragon and Saint George have joined forces and are beating up on the referee! Sit down and listen. Wow!"

The Little Red Hen didn't like the sound of that at all, so she scurried away to the mill. Mickey Mouse was glad to grind the wheat, and she left the mill with just enough flour for a fine loaf of bread.

She wandered around asking, "Who will help me bake my bread?" But nobody was interested, so she did it herself. When she took the loaf from the oven, she put it on the windowsill to cool.

At this moment who should come strolling down the lane but Gladstone Gander, who was known far and wide as one lucky duck. He was in costume to try out for the lead in *The Student Prince*, soon to be presented by the Duckville Summer Hiking and Theater Society.

He smelled the bread cooling on the windowsill, and he said to himself, "Gladstone, you lucky duck, some kind soul has put this loaf of bread on the window for you to eat. How lucky can you get?" He took the loaf of bread and sat down to enjoy it.

But the Little Red Hen didn't see Gladstone Gander. Thinking that her loaf of bread was safe, she ran to her friends. "Who will help me eat my bread?" she asked.

Gus Goose leaped up from his resting place. "Vacation's over," he announced happily. "Time for a little old-fashioned bread eating."

Donald Duck was in the middle of a *trippity-boom* when he heard Little Red Hen

call out. He dropped the bongos immediately and ran toward the house. "Chickie-baby, I'm with you," he said. And though her name wasn't Chickie-baby, the Little Red Hen was quite pleased. She liked to have company.

The Duck nephews heard the glad words above the blare of their transistor, and they turned it off. "Dragon fight's over," they shouted. "Time for some bread and jam."

Soon they were all at the Little Red Hen's house—all except the loaf of bread. "Where is the bread?" they all asked together.

Then they all saw Gladstone Gander licking his fingers. Donald pointed to Gladstone. "There is the luckiest Duck in the valley."

"In the *world*," added Gus Goose.

The Little Red Hen was overjoyed. Her bread had been eaten by a prince. She recognized him immediately.

"You," she said, "are a prince. You have come to give me treasure—rubies and diamonds and sapphires and emeralds."

"Who?" Gladstone asked. "Me?"

"Of course you. You're a prince, aren't you?"

"As a matter of fact, I'm an out-of-work actor," said Gladstone.

Everybody looked at Gladstone, then they all looked at the Little Red Hen. They all wondered what she would do. After a while she shrugged and said, "Well, you can't win 'em all."

The Reluctant Dragon

Long ago—it might have been hundreds of years ago—in a cottage halfway between this village and yonder shoulder of the Downs up there, a shepherd lived with his wife and their little son. Now the shepherd spent his days—and at certain times of the year his nights too—up on the wide ocean-bosom of the Downs, with only the sun and the stars and the sheep for company, and the friendly chattering world of men and women far out of sight and hearing. But his little son, when he wasn't helping his father, and often when he was as well, spent much of his time buried in big books that he borrowed from the affable gentry and interested parsons of the country round about.

One day the boy was reading, as usual, when his father, the shepherd, came running up all out of breath.

"It's horrible, Son!" cried the shepherd. "I saw it! Halfway out of his hole he was, and covered with scales and such like. And a tail with sort of a hook on it!"

The boy did not even look up from his book. "It's only a dragon, Father," he said.

"Only a dragon!" shouted the shepherd.

"Don't worry, Father," said the boy calmly. "I'll have a look at him, soon as I've finished this chapter."

But the father ran off toward the village shouting, "Help! Everybody lock your doors! Help! A dragon's coming!"

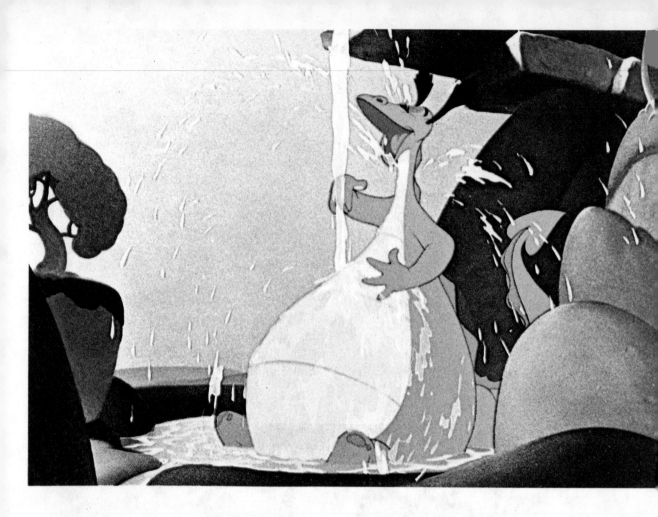

The boy quietly finished his chapter. Then after he'd had his tea, he strolled up the chalky track that led to the summit of the Downs. There, sure enough, he found the dragon.

The dragon was taking a bath and singing happily to himself.

"Ahem," said the boy. "Hello, Dragon."

The dragon was a bit startled, and more than a bit suspicious. "Now, Boy," he warned, "don't bung stones at me or squirt water or anything. I won't have it."

"Oh, I just came up for a friendly chat," said the boy, "but if I'm not wanted—"

At that, the dragon remembered his manners. "Do be seated," he told the boy. "But if you don't mind, look the other way, please. I'll only be a minute."

So the boy looked the other way as the dragon finished his bath. Then he asked if the dragon had had any nice battles of late.

"Battles?" The dragon shook his head. "No. No battles."

"Oh!" said the boy. "Too busy scourging the countryside and devouring fair damsels, eh?"

"Scourging?" exclaimed the dragon. "Devouring. Good heavens, no!"

"But don't you ever do anything desperate?" asked the boy.

"Well, yes!" said the dragon. "I do make up poetry."

"Poetry?" The boy was disappointed.

"Verses, you know," explained the dragon. "Care to hear my latest sonnet?"

The boy didn't really, but he didn't want to be rude and say so right out.

"You'll love this," said the dragon happily. "I call it, 'Just a-Drifting.'"

Then the dragon began to recite:

"Just a-drifting o'er the lea,
Like a dewdrop, fancy free.
Playing with the gentle breezes
Romping with the bumble beezes
Oh what fun—joy never ceases
Just a-drifting—"

The boy felt that poetry might be all very well, but he had more important things to discuss with the dragon.

"Very nice," he said, "but you're in for trouble, you know."

"Trouble?" echoed the dragon.

"You're a pest and a baneful monster," said the boy.

"Not a word of truth in that! My character will bear the strictest investigation."

And the dragon went on with his poem:

"Prancing, dancing to and fro—
Not too fast—not too slow,
Where the early birds are seeking,

Early worms who slyly peeking,
Hear the night owls softly shrieking,
Just a-drifting."

"But you don't understand," said the boy. "My father's arousing the village, and they'll be here with spears and things to exterminate you! You're an enemy of the human race."

But the dragon was so entranced with his poetry that he didn't become the least bit aroused. Ho-o-oh! I haven't an enemy in the world," he declared. "Too lazy to make them."

He kept on reciting happily, swaying back and forth in time to the rhythm of the words.

The boy got up. "If you won't be sensible, I'm going off home. I'll look you up tomorrow, sometime or other, and do for goodness' sake try and realize that you're a pestilential scourge, or you'll find yourself in a most awful fix."

And what the boy feared soon came to pass. The most modest and retiring dragon in the world, if he's as big as four cart horses and covered with scales, cannot keep altogether out of the public view. And so, in the village, the fact that a real live dragon sat brooding in the cave on the Downs was naturally a subject for talk. Though the villagers were extremely frightened, they were rather proud as well. It was a distinction to have a dragon of your own, and it was felt to be a feather in the cap of the village. Still, all were agreed that this sort of thing couldn't be allowed to go on. The dreadful beast must be exterminated. The countryside must be freed from this pest, this terror, this destroying scourge.

The fact that not even a hen roost was the worse for the dragon's arrival wasn't allowed to have anything to do with it. He was a dragon, and he couldn't deny it, and

if he didn't choose to behave as such, that was his own lookout.

But in spite of such valiant talk, no hero was found willing to take sword and spear and free the suffering village and win deathless fame. So the dragon lolled on the turf, enjoying the sunsets. He told old tales to the boy, polished his old verses, and thought about new ones.

One day the boy went into the village and found everything looking very festive. Carpets and bright banners were hung from the windows. The church bells clamored noisily, and the little street was strewn with flowers. The whole population jostled each other along either side of the street, chattering and shoving and ordering each other to stand back.

As the boy stared and wondered, the people began to shout.

"Here he comes now!"

"Oh, isn't he handsome!"

"He's a spectacle, he is!"

"Hey!" cried the boy. "What's all the excitement?"

"It's Sir Giles, stupid!" said one man. "Hooray! Hooray for Sir Giles! Hooray for the dragon-killer!"

Presently, from the faraway end of the line came the sound of more cheering. Next, the measured tramp of a great war-horse made the boy's heart beat quicker. Then he found himself cheering with the rest, as, amidst welcoming shouts, shrill cries of women, uplifting of babies, and waving of handkerchiefs, Sir Giles paced slowly up the street. The boy's heart stood still and he

breathed with sobs; the beauty and the grace of the hero were so far beyond anything he had yet seen. His fluted armor was inlaid with gold. His plumed helmet hung at his saddlebow, and his thick, fair hair framed a face gracious and gentle beyond expression —till you caught the sternness in his eyes. He drew rein in front of the little inn, and the villagers crowded around with greetings and thanks and voluble statements of their wrongs and grievances and oppressions.

The boy heard the grave, gentle voice of the knight assuring them that all would be well now, and that he would stand by them and see them righted and free them from their foe. Then he dismounted and passed through the doorway, and the crowd poured in after him.

But the boy made off up the hill as fast as he could lay his feet to the ground. As

soon as he was within sight of the dragon, the boy began to shout.

"It's all up, Dragon! He's coming. He's here now!"

The dragon, who had been reciting verses as usual, spoke in cool tones. "Now, Boy, it's impolite to interrupt a person. Who's coming?"

"Sir Giles, on a big horse, with a long sword and a spear, and you'll have to fight him."

"I never fight," said the dragon. "Never did. Doesn't agree with me."

"But—but—but—"

"Now, Boy, just run along. Tell Sir Giles to go away. I'm sure you can arrange it."

The boy made his way back to the village in a state of great distress. His dear and honored friend the dragon hadn't shown up in a heroic light. Also, whether the dragon was a hero or not, it made no difference, for Sir Giles would most undoubtedly cut his head off.

"Arrange things indeed!" he said bitterly to himself. "The dragon treats the whole affair as if it were an invitation to tea and croquet."

The villagers were straggling homewards as the boy passed up the street. All of them were in the highest spirits, and gleefully discussing the splendid fight that was in store. The boy went into the inn, found Sir Giles' room, and paused at the door. The knight was busily engaged with a scrubbing sponge.

"Excuse me, Sir," said the boy. "You are Sir Giles, I presume?"

The knight looked up and spoke in a kindly voice. "Come, come, lad. Stop mumbling."

"I came to talk about the dragon," said the boy.

"Ah, yes!" said the knight. "Another tale of woe and misery. Devoured your flocks, no doubt?"

"Oh, no Sir!" said the boy.

"Aha!" cried the knight. "Made off with your loving parents, has he?"

"You don't understand—"

"What! Don't tell me he's kidnapped some fair damsel with flaxen hair, ruby lips, ivory skin! Why, he can't do that! He shall pay dearly on the field of battle!"

"But that's just it," said the boy. "He won't fight!"

"He what? He won't fight? Preposterous! Fellow must be an infernal cad!"

The boy rushed to his friend's defense. "He is not a cad. He's a nice old dragon who likes to write poetry."

"Poetry?" said the knight.

"Yes. Verses, you know."

The knight brightened up. "By Jove! How jolly! I'm a bit of a poet myself, you know."

The boy was astonished. "You, a poet, too?"

"Yes. No doubt you've heard of my 'Ode to a Fleecy Cloud.'"

The boy hadn't, and the knight began to recite it:

> "Oh fleecy cloud
> Oh cloud of fleece
> Up in the sky so high
> Oh—
> Oh my—"

The knight interrupted himself. "But come. Let's not dillydally. We must meet this fine fellow at once."

"Then you'll explain to the dragon about the fight?"

"Yes. Quite so." The knight quickly dried himself and put on his clothes. "You're taking a lot of trouble on your friend's account," he said good-naturedly as he and the boy went out together. "Cheer up! Perhaps there won't have to be any fight after all."

That wasn't exactly what the boy wanted. He knew the villagers were looking forward to a fight. They demanded a fight. They would never be satisfied until there was a fight.

The boy himself thought that a battle between the knight and the dragon would be only proper. Tradition demanded it.

But the boy said nothing, and when he and the knight arrived at the cave, he greeted the dragon first. "Hello, Dragon," he said.

"Hello, Boy," answered the dragon. "I'm having a picnic. Won't you join me?"

"Well," said the boy, "I brought a friend to explain—"

"Splendid!" cried the dragon. "The more the merrier. Now, Boy, you sit here, and your friend can sit there. Let's see now. Pickles, jam, muffins, tea. Ah, yes. Here, do have a sandwich, Sir—ah—Sir—ah—"

"This *is* jolly!" said Sir Giles.

"What did you say your friend's name was?" the dragon whispered to the boy.

"That's Sir Giles," answered the boy. "Sir Giles, the dragon-killer."

"Sir Giles?" cried the dragon.

"Ah, yes," said the knight. "I've been looking forward to meeting you. The boy here tells me you're quite an accomplished poet."

"He did? Really?" The dragon seemed very pleased to hear this.

"Yes. And if it's not too much bother, I'd be happy to hear you recite."

"Oh, my dear fellow," said the dragon. "No bother. No bother at all. Would you care for another sandwich? And a piece of cake? How about a crumpet and a spot of tea?"

"Thank you," mumbled the knight whose mouth was full of food.

"This is called, 'To an Upside-Down Cake.'" announced the dragon, and he cleared his throat and began:

"Sweet little Upside-Down Cake,
Cares and woes, you've gotten
Poor little Upside-Down Cake,
Your top is on your bottom.
Alas, little Upside-Down Cake,
Your troubles never stop,
Because, little Upside-Down Cake,
Your bottom's on your top."

130

"Bravo!" applauded Sir Giles. "How interesting! Extraordinary!"

The boy felt quite uneasy. He thought they should be getting to the point. "Sir Giles, tell the dragon *now!*" he urged.

"Ah, yes," said Sir Giles. "You know, I'm a bit of a bard myself."

"Not really?" said the dragon.

The knight proved it. He recited a little verse he had composed in praise of a radish:

> "*Radish so red,*
> *Radish so red,*
> *Plucked from the heart*
> *Of your warm little bed.*
> *Sprinkled with salt*
> *On the top of your head—*
> *Delicious!*"

The dragon declared the poem exquisite.

The boy didn't like the way things were going at all. He decided to take things into his own hands. "Do you mind if I recite a poem?"

The dragon didn't, nor did Sir Giles, so the boy began:

> "*'Tis evening—*
> *From the stars above*
> *A soft, mysterious light*
> *Brings thoughts of friendship,*
> *Joy, and love—*
> *Now how about that fight??!*"

"Fight? There's nothing to fight about. Besides, I don't believe in it!" said the dragon.

The boy knew that wasn't quite the point. "Dragons and knights always fight," he explained. "Besides, you can't disappoint the whole village."

"Hm!" said Sir Giles. "The lad's right. Not cricket, you know."

But the dragon absolutely refused to discuss it. He absolutely refused to fight.

"Y'know, it's a shame," said the knight. "It doesn't seem right. This is really a beautiful spot for a fight."

The boy could almost see it—with flags

waving and people cheering and bands playing.

"The dragon appears," said Sir Giles. "What a beautiful sight, with his scales all a-gleam in the dawn's early light!"

"You're just flattering me!" said the dragon.

"No, old fellow, it's true!" said the knight, and then he told how a beautiful damsel would doubtless throw flowers at the dragon. It would all be terribly exciting.

"Look! Here comes Sir Giles on his milky-white horse, shouting his battle cry, waving his spear," said the boy.

"Spear?" exclaimed the dragon. "Oh! Oh, dear! I'll get hurt. I won't do it!"

"Just a second, old chap," said the knight. "We might fix it this way."

And the knight whispered to the dragon.

"You mean it?" said the dragon, and he whispered to the knight.

"Quite so!" declared the knight. He winked at the dragon.

"Good show!" exclaimed the dragon. He winked at the knight. "But are you sure it's quite honest?"

The knight happened to have an official

book of battle rules in his pocket. He took it out and looked into it. "Nothing against it here," he said cheerfully.

"Very well, then. It's settled," said the dragon. "Tomorrow we fight."

Sir Giles and the boy started back toward the village, and the dragon chuckled to himself.

"There's going to be a fight! There's going to be a fight. A fight?" The dragon stopped chuckling. "Oh! Oh, wait! Oh, no! Oh, I can't! Oh, why don't I keep my big mouth shut?"

The next morning, the people began streaming up to the Downs at quite an early hour. They wore their Sunday clothes and carried baskets with bottlenecks sticking out of them. Everyone was intent on getting a good place to watch the combat.

But things were in a terrible state inside the dragon's cave. The dragon was in despair and the boy didn't know what to do to help the situation.

"It's no use," said the dragon. "You might as well tell the people to go away. I can't do it."

"Try again," begged the boy.

"But you've got to be mad to breathe fire," said the dragon, "and I'm not mad at anybody."

"Maybe if you try real hard," said the boy. "Concentrate!"

The dragon tried very hard indeed. With a terrific effort, he managed to cough out a tiny puff of smoke and a small weak flame. He looked at the boy apologetically.

"Not very good, is it?"

"Terrible," said the boy. Then he almost smiled, and then he scowled. "Too bad you're not a real dragon, instead of a punk poet."

"*Punk poet?*" cried the dragon. "Say that again!"

The boy said it again—and again and again. "PUNK POET! PUNK POET! PUNK POET!"

As the insulting words lashed at him, the dragon became a fearful sight. Clouds of black smoke and long tongues of flame shot from his throat.

"WHOO-WHOO! I'M MAD!" shouted the dragon.

The boy was delighted.

By now, the higher portions of the ground were black with sightseers. Presently there was a cheering and a waving of handkerchiefs. A minute more and Sir Giles' red plumes topped the hill as the knight rode slowly forth on the great level space which stretched up to the grim mouth of the cave. Very gallant and beautiful he looked on his tall warhorse, his armor glancing in the sun, his great spear held erect, the little white pennon, crimson-crossed, fluttering at its point. He drew rein and remained motionless. The lines of spectators began to give back a little nervously. Even the boys in front stopped pulling hair and cuffing each other and leaned forward.

A low muttering, mingled with snorts, now made itself heard. It rose to a bellowing roar that seemed to fill the plain. Then a cloud of smoke hid the mouth of the cave, and out of the smoke came the dragon himself.

Shining, sea-blue and magnificent, he pranced splendidly forth. Everybody said, "Oo-oo-oh!" as if he had been a mighty rocket. His scales

were glittering. His long spiky tail lashed his sides. His claws tore up the turf and sent it flying high over his back, and smoke and fire jetted from his angry nostrils.

The knight was amazed. By Jove, that dragon was playing his part with all the fire at his command.

"Boo!" roared the dragon at the crowd. "Boo! Boo! Boo!" He blew out great smoke rings. Then he disappeared behind a rock.

"Dragon! I say, Dragon!" called Sir Giles.

The dragon peeked out playfully. He was most pleased with himself. "How am I doing?" he asked.

"I say, old boy, stop acting so silly, will you?" pleaded the knight. "I mean, this is serious business, you know."

So the dragon obligingly changed his mood. He began screaming as though he were terribly afraid of Sir Giles. "Help! Help! Oh, help!"

He then darted into his cave. Sir Giles

went after him, and the delighted crowd heard what seemed to be a violent battle going on. Groans and shouts and cries for help issued from the cave. But inside, the boy was seeing something very different from a battle to the death. The dragon was serving tea for Sir Giles, while both of them screamed and yelled for the benefit of the crowd outside.

"Ouch!" shouted the dragon. "One lump or two?"

"You bounder!" screamed the knight. "Two if you don't mind."

"HELP! HELP! HELP!" cried the dragon, and he handed the cup to Sir Giles.

They drank their tea, with the knight shouting insults and the dragon giving great

howls of pain between sips. When they had finished, Sir Giles put down his cup.

"Now I'll chase you," he told the dragon.

"Capital!" exclaimed the dragon, and he ran out of the cave with the enthusiastic knight at his heels and the boy running after them. And out on the Downs, the fight went on amid clouds of smoke and flashes of flame and pounding of hoofs.

At last, the knight gave the word. "Sorry, old chap. It's been jolly fun, but the time has come, you know."

"You mean, you vanquish me now?" asked the dragon.

"Yes, indeed. As we agreed," said the knight.

a good time to eat, everyone got out their baskets and started to picnic.

After refreshments, Sir Giles made a speech. He informed his audience that he had removed their direful scourge, at a great deal

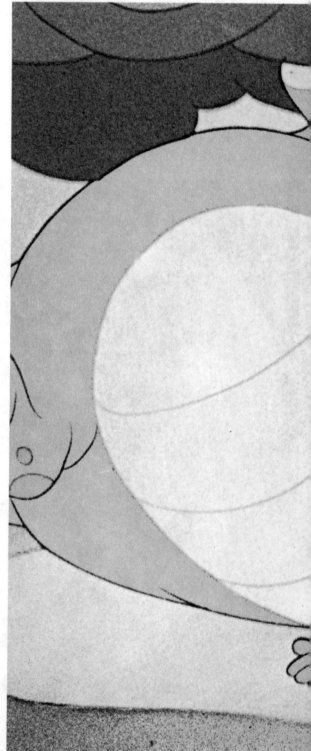

So the dragon stopped dashing about and ranting and roaring and the knight pricked him, ever so carefully, in a place they had both agreed upon.

"Oh death, where is they sting?" moaned the dragon. He gave a last yell, then rolled over on the ground. The knight dismounted and put his foot on the dragon's neck.

It looked so real that the boy ran to them breathlessly.

"Dragon! Dragon, speak to me. Are you all right?"

As the boy approached, the dragon lifted one large eyelid and winked solemnly. He was held fast to the earth by the neck, but he was not even slightly uncomfortable. The knight had hit him so skillfully that it hadn't even tickled.

"Aren't you going to cut his head off, master?" asked one of the applauding crowd.

"Well, not today, I think," replied Sir Giles pleasantly. "You see, I can cut his head off at any time. There's no hurry at all. I'll give him a good talking-to, and you'll find he'll be a very different dragon!"

Sir Giles began to talk very earnestly and very quietly to the dragon, and as it seemed of trouble and inconvenience to himself, and now they weren't to go about grumbling and fancying they had grievances, because they hadn't.

Then he told them that the dragon had been thinking things over and saw that there were two sides to every question, and he wasn't going to do it any more, and if they were good perhaps he'd stay and settle down there. So they must make friends, and not

be prejudiced, and go about fancying they knew everything there was to be known, because they didn't, not by a long way.

Whereupon the dragon felt called upon to make a speech too:

"Cross my heart and hope to die,
I'm a reformed dragon, aren't I?
I promise not to rant and roar
And scourge the countryside, any more."

"Hear hear!" said the crowd.

"And I propose a toast to the boy!" said the dragon.

The crowd cheered.

"I propose a toast to every member of the crowd," suggested the knight. "The toasts to be drunk separately, of course!"

This was such a wonderful idea that the villagers cheered until they were hoarse. Then they packed the remains of their picnic lunches into their baskets and they all trooped back to the inn, which was the only proper place for quite so many toasts.

The celebration took a very long time indeed, and it was late when the villagers straggled off to their homes. The knight and the dragon and the boy started back to the cave. The lights in the village began to go out, but there were stars and a late moon. The poetic spell of the night took hold of them, and the knight and the dragon began to recite:

> *"Oh moon of cheese—*
> *Oh cheesy moon—*
> *Up in the sky so clear—*
> *Oh—*
> *Oh dear—"*

And, as they climbed the Downs together and disappeared from view, snatches of an old song were borne back on the night breeze. I can't be certain which of them was singing, but I think it was the dragon!

Everyone cheered. Then the knight rose again. "I propose a toast to the dragon!"

"Hear hear!" shouted the crowd.

"I propose a toast to the knight!" said the boy.

Alice in Wonderland

Alice was beginning to get very tired of sitting by her sister and of having nothing to do. Now and then she petted her cat Dinah, and once or twice she peeped into the book her sister was reading, but it had no pictures or conversations in it, "and what is the use of a book," thought Alice, "without pictures or conversations?"

So she was considering, in her own mind (as well as she could, for the hot day made her feel very sleepy), whether the pleasure of making a daisy chain would be worth the trouble of picking the daisies, when suddenly a White Rabbit with pink eyes ran close by her.

"Oh, dear! Oh, dear!" said the Rabbit to himself. "I shall be too late!" And the Rabbit took a watch out of his waistcoat pocket, and looked at it, and then hurried on. Alice started to her feet, for it flashed across her mind that she had never before seen a rabbit with either a waistcoat pocket or a watch to take

out of it, and, burning with curiosity, she ran across the field after him, and was just in time to see him pop down a large rabbit hole under the hedge.

In another moment down went Alice after the rabbit, never once considering how in the world she was to get out again.

The rabbit hole went straight on like a tunnel for some way, and then dipped suddenly down, so suddenly that Alice had not a moment to think about stopping herself before she found herself falling down what seemed to be a very deep well.

Down, down, down she went. Would the fall *never* come to an end? After a time she said aloud, "I wonder how many miles I've fallen. I must be getting somewhere near the center of the earth. I wonder if I shall fall right through the earth!"

Down, down, down. As there was nothing else to do, Alice went on talking. "Dinah'll miss me very much tonight, I should think!

I hope they'll remember her saucer of milk at tea time. Dinah, my dear! I wish you were down here with me. There are no mice in the air, I'm afraid, but you might catch a bat, and that's very like a mouse, you know. But do cats eat bats, I wonder?" And here Alice began to get rather sleepy, and went on saying to herself in a dreamy sort of way, "Do cats eat bats? Do cats eat bats?" And sometimes, "Do bats eat cats?" She felt that she was dozing off when suddenly, thump! thump! and the fall was over.

Alice was not a bit hurt, and she jumped to her feet in a moment. She looked up, but it was all dark overhead. The White Rabbit was still in sight, hurrying along and saying, "Oh my ears and whiskers, how late it's getting!" All at once he pulled aside a curtain and disappeared through a little door about fifteen inches high.

Alice looked around. She was in a long, low hall, which was lit up by a row of lamps hanging from the roof. She saw a little three-legged table, with a solid glass top. On it was a tiny golden key. Alice pulled aside the curtain in front of the little door and tried the golden key in the lock. To her great delight it fitted!

Alice opened the door and found that it led into a small passage. She knelt down and looked along the passage into the loveliest garden you ever saw. How she longed to get out of that dark hall, and wander about among those beds of bright flowers and those cool fountains, but she could not even get her head through the doorway. "And even if my head *would* go through," thought poor Alice, "it would be of very little use without my shoulders. Oh, how I wish I could shut up like a telescope!"

There seemed to be no use in waiting by the little door, so she went back to the table. This time she found a little bottle on it, and tied round the neck of the bottle was a paper label, with the words "DRINK ME" beautifully printed on it in large letters.

Alice opened the bottle, and she ventured to taste what was in it. It was something very nice. It had, in fact, a sort of mixed flavor of cherry tart, custard, pineapple, roast turkey, toffy, and hot buttered toast. She very soon finished it off.

And, "What a curious feeling!" said Alice. "I must be shutting up like a telescope!"

And so it was indeed. She was now only ten inches high, and her face brightened up at the thought that she was now the right size for going through the little door into that lovely garden.

Alas for poor Alice! When she got to the door, she found she had forgotten the little golden key, and when she went back to the table for it, she found she could not possibly reach it. She could see it quite plainly through the glass, and she tried her best to climb up one of the legs of the table, but it was too slippery. When she had tired herself out with trying, the poor little thing sat down and cried.

But soon her eye fell on a little box that was lying under the table. She opened it, and found in it a very small cake, on which the words "EAT ME" were beautifully marked in currants. "Well, I'll eat it," said Alice, "and if it makes me grow larger, I can reach the key. If it makes me grow smaller, I can creep under the door, so either way I'll get into the garden, and I don't care which happens!"

So she set to work, and very soon finished off the cake.

"Curiouser and curiouser!" cried Alice. "Now I'm opening out like the largest telescope that ever was!"

Just at this moment her head struck against the roof of the hall. In fact she was rather more than nine feet high, and she at once took up the little golden key and hurried off to the garden door.

Poor Alice! It was as much as she could do, lying down on one side, to look through into the garden with one eye. To get through was more hopeless than ever. She sat down and began to cry again. She shed gallons

of tears, until there was a large pool all round her, about four inches deep, and reaching half down the hall.

After a time she heard a little pattering of feet, and she hastily dried her eyes to see what was coming. It was the White Rabbit, splendidly dressed, with a pair of white kid gloves in one hand and a large fan in the other. He came trotting along in a great hurry, muttering to himself, "Oh! Oh, my ears and whiskers, but I'm late!"

"If you please, Sir—," said Alice.

The Rabbit started violently, dropped the white kid gloves and the fan, and scurried away into the darkness as hard as he could go.

Alice took up the fan and gloves. "Dear, dear! How queer everything is today!" she said. "And yesterday things went on just as usual. I wonder if I've been changed in the night? Let me think. *Was* I the same when I got up this morning? I almost think I can remember feeling a little different."

As she said this she looked down at her hands, and was surprised to see that she had put on one of the Rabbit's little white kid gloves while she was talking. "How *can* I have done that?" she thought. "I must be growing small again." And she was. She was about two feet high, and was shrinking rapidly. She soon found out that the cause of this was the fan she was holding, and she dropped it hastily, just in time to save herself from shrinking away altogether.

"That *was* a narrow escape!" said Alice, very glad to find herself still in existence. "And now for the garden!" And she ran with all speed back to the little door. But, alas! The little door was shut again, and the little golden key was lying on the glass table as before. "And things are worse than ever," thought Alice, "for I never was so small as this before!"

As she said these words her foot slipped, and in another moment, splash! She was up to her chin in salt water. Her first idea was that she had somehow fallen into the sea. However, she soon made out that she

was in the pool of tears which she had wept when she was nine feet high. The pool was quite crowded with birds and animals that had fallen into it. There was a Duck and a Dodo, a Lory and an Eaglet, and several other curious creatures. Alice led the way, and the whole party got to the shore.

They were indeed a queer-looking party that assembled on the bank—the birds with draggled feathers, the animals with their fur clinging close to them, and all dripping wet, cross, and uncomfortable.

The first question of course, was, how to get dry again. They had a consultation about this, and after a few minutes it seemed quite natural to Alice to find herself talking familiarly with them, as if she had known them all her life.

"What I say," announced the Dodo, "is that the best way to get us dry would be a Caucus-race."

"What *is* a Caucus-race?" said Alice.

"Why," said the Dodo, "the best way to explain it is to do it." (And, as you might like to try the thing yourself some winter day, I will tell you how the Dodo managed it.)

First it marked out a race course, in a sort of circle, and then all the party were placed along the course, here and there. There was no "One, two, three, and away!" but they began running when they liked and left off when they liked, so that it was not easy to know when the race was over. However, when they had been running half an hour or so, and were quite dry again, the Dodo suddenly called out, "The race is over!" They all crowded round it, panting, and asking, "But who has won?"

The Dodo stood for a long time with one finger pressed upon its forehead, while the rest waited in silence. At last the Dodo said, "*Everybody* has won, and *all* must have prizes."

"But who is to give the prizes?" quite a chorus of voices asked.

"Why, *she,* of course," said the Dodo, pointing to Alice.

Alice put her hand in her pocket, and pulled out a box of comfits. (Luckily the salt water had not got into it.) She handed them round as prizes. There was exactly one apiece, all round.

And, since all the animals insisted that she must have a prize herself, she put her hand in her pocket and pulled out a thimble and gave it to the Dodo.

Then they all crowded round her while the Dodo solemnly presented the thimble, saying, "We beg your acceptance of this elegant thimble." When it had finished this short speech, they all cheered.

The next thing was to eat the comfits. This caused some noise and confusion, as the large birds complained that they could not taste theirs, and the small ones choked and had to be patted on the back. However, it was over at last, and they all sat down in a ring.

"I wish I had our Dinah here, I know I do," said Alice, addressing nobody in particular.

"And who is Dinah, if I might venture to ask the question?" said the Lory.

Alice replied eagerly, for she was always ready to talk about her pet: "Dinah's our cat. And she's such a capital one for catching mice, you can't think! And oh, I wish you could see her after the birds!"

This speech caused a remarkable sensation among the party. Some of the birds hurried off at once. One old Magpie began wrapping itself up very carefully, remarking, "I really must be getting home. The night air doesn't suit my throat!" And a Canary called out in a trembling voice, to its children, "Come away, my dears! It's high time you were all in bed!" On various pretexts they all moved off, and Alice was soon left alone.

And here poor Alice began to cry again, for she felt very lonely and low-spirited. In a little while, however, she again heard a little pattering of footsteps in the distance, and she looked up eagerly.

It was the White Rabbit, trotting slowly back again, and looking anxiously about as he went, as if he had lost something.

Alice guessed in a moment that he was looking for the fan and the pair of white kid gloves. She very good-naturedly began hunting about for them, but they were nowhere to be seen.

Everything seemed to have changed since her swim in the pool, and the great hall, with the glass table and the little door, had vanished completely.

After following the Rabbit for only a short distance, they came to a neat little house.

thing interesting is sure to happen," she said to herself, "whenever I eat or drink anything, so I'll just see what this cookie does. I do hope it'll make me grow large again, for really I'm quite tired of being such a tiny little thing!"

It did so indeed, and much sooner than she had expected. Before she had half finished it, she found her head pressing against the ceiling. She went on growing and growing until, as a last resource, she put her arms out of the window. Then she said to herself, "Now I can do no more, whatever happens. What *will* become of me?"

Luckily for Alice, the little magic cookie had now had its full effect, and she grew no larger. Still it was very uncomfortable, and, as there seemed to be no sort of chance of her ever getting out of the room again, no wonder she felt unhappy.

"Mary Ann! Mary Ann!" said a voice. "Fetch me my gloves this moment!" Then came a little pattering of feet outside. Alice knew it was the Rabbit, coming to look for her.

"What's that in the window?" cried the Rabbit.

"Sure, it's an arm." Alice recognized the voice of the Dodo.

"Well, it's got no business there," declared the Rabbit, and after a minute or two Alice heard someone moving about.

"A barrowfull will do, to begin with," said the Rabbit.

"A barrowfull of *what*?" thought Alice. But she had not long to doubt, for the next moment a shower of little pebbles came rattling in at the window, and some of them hit her in the face. "I'll put a stop to this," she said to herself, and shouted out, "You'd better not do that again!" This produced a dead silence.

Alice noticed, with some surprise, that the pebbles were all turning into little cakes as they lay on the floor, and a bright idea came into her head. "If I eat one of these cakes," she thought, "it's sure to make *some*

The Rabbit noticed Alice, as she went hunting about, and called out to her in an angry tone, "Why, Mary Ann, what are you doing out here? Run into the house this moment, and fetch me a pair of gloves and a fan! Quick now!"

"He took me for his housemaid," said Alice to herself and, without trying to explain the mistake that the rabbit had made, she ran into the house. She hurried upstairs, in great fear lest she should meet the real Mary Ann, and be turned out of the house before she had found the fan and gloves.

She found her way into a tidy little room containing a dresser, a rocking chair, and a table near the window. She looked about for the gloves and fan, but could not find them. She was just going to leave the room when her eye fell upon a jar which contained some cookies. She took one. "I know *some-*

change in my size, and, as it can't possibly make me larger, it must make me smaller, I suppose."

So she swallowed one of the cakes, and was delighted to find that she began shrinking directly. As soon as she was small enough to get through the door, she ran out of the house and found quite a crowd of little animals and birds waiting outside. Alice ran off as quickly as she could, and soon was safe in a thick wood.

"The first thing I've got to do," said Alice to herself, as she wandered about, "is to grow to my right size again, and the second thing is to find my way into that lovely garden. I think that will be the best plan."

It sounded an excellent plan, no doubt, and very neatly and simply arranged. The only difficulty was that she had not the smallest idea how to set about it. "I suppose I ought to eat or drink something or other," said Alice, "but the great question is, 'What?'"

The great question certainly was "What?" Alice looked all round her at the flowers and the blades of grass, but she could not see anything that looked like the right thing to eat or drink under the circumstances.

She went on and on until she came to a large mushroom. It was about the same height as herself, and, when she had looked under it and on both sides of it and behind it, it occurred to her that she might as well look and see what was on the top of it.

She stretched herself up on tiptoe, and peeped over the edge of the mushroom, and her eyes immediately met those of a large caterpillar that was sitting on the top, with its arms folded, quietly smoking a water pipe.

"Who are *you*?" asked the Caterpillar.

Alice replied, rather shyly, "I—I hardly know, Sir, just at present—at least I know who I *was* when I got up this morning, but I think I must have been changed several times since then."

"What do you mean by that?" said the Caterpillar, sternly. "Explain yourself."

"I can't explain *myself*, I'm afraid, Sir," said Alice, "because I'm not myself, you see."

"I don't see," said the Caterpillar.

"I'm afraid I can't put it more clearly," Alice replied, very politely. "Being so many different sizes in a day is very confusing."

"It isn't," said the Caterpillar.

"Well, perhaps you haven't found it so

yet," said Alice, "but when you have to turn into a chrysalis—you will some day, you know—and then after that into a butterfly, I should think you'll feel it a little queer, won't you?"

"Not a bit," said the Caterpillar.

"It would feel very queer to me," said Alice, and, as the Caterpillar seemed to be in a *very* unpleasant state of mind, she turned away.

"Come back!" the Caterpillar called after her. "I've something important to say!"

This sounded promising, certainly. Alice turned and came back again.

"Keep your temper," said the Caterpillar.

"Is that all?"

"No," said the Caterpillar. "What size do you want to be?"

"Oh, I'm not particular as to size," Alice hastily replied, "only one doesn't like changing so often, you know."

"I *don't* know," said the Caterpillar.

Alice said nothing.

"Are you content now?" said the Caterpillar.

"Well, I should like to be a *little* larger, Sir, if you wouldn't mind," said Alice. "Three inches is such a wretched height to be."

"It is a very good height indeed!" said the Caterpillar angrily, rearing itself upright as it spoke. (It was exactly three inches high.)

"But I'm not used to it!" pleaded Alice. The Caterpillar yawned once or twice, then got down off the mushroom and crawled away into the grass, merely remarking as it went, "One side will make you grow taller, and the other side will make you grow shorter."

"One side of what?" thought Alice to herself.

"Of the mushroom," said the Caterpillar, just as if she had asked it aloud. And in another moment it was out of sight.

Alice looked thoughtfully at the mushroom for a minute, trying to make out which were the two sides of it. As it was perfectly round, she found this a very difficult question. However, at last she stretched her arms round it as far as they would go, and broke off a bit of the edge with each hand.

"And now which is which?" she said to herself, and nibbled a little of the right-hand bit to try the effect.

In a moment, she found that her shoulders were nowhere to be found. All she could see, when she looked down, was an immense length of neck which seemed to rise like a stalk out of a sea of green leaves that lay far below her.

"What *can* all that green stuff be?" said Alice. "And where *have* my shoulders got to? And my poor hands, how is it I can't see you?"

As there seemed to be no chance of getting her hands up to her head, she tried to get her head down to *them*, and was delighted to find that her neck would bend easily. She was just going to dive in among the leaves, which she found to be nothing but the tops of the trees under which she had been wandering, when a sharp hiss made her draw back in a hurry. A little bird had flown into her face and was beating her violently with its wings.

"Serpent!" screamed the Bird.

"I'm *not* a serpent!" said Alice indignantly. "Let me alone!"

"Serpent, I say again!" repeated the Bird, but in a more subdued tone.

"But I'm *not* a serpent, I tell you!" said Alice. "I'm a—I'm a—"

"Well! *What* are you?" said the Bird. "I—I'm a little girl," said Alice, rather doubtfully, as she remembered the number of changes she had gone through that day.

"A likely story indeed!" said the Bird, in a tone of the deepest contempt. "I've seen a good many little girls in my time, but never *one* with such a neck as that! You're a serpent and you're looking for eggs. I know *that* well enough."

"I'm not looking for eggs, as it happens," said Alice hastily, "and, if I was, I wouldn't want *yours*. I don't like them raw."

"Well, be off, then!" said the Bird in a

sulky tone, as it settled down into its nest. Alice crouched down among the trees, and after a while she remembered that she still held the pieces of mushroom in her hands. She set to work very carefully, nibbling first at one and then at the other, and growing sometimes taller, and sometimes shorter, until she had succeeded in bringing herself down to her usual height.

It was so long since she had been anything near the right size that it felt quite strange at first, but she got used to it in a few minutes and began talking to herself. "Come, there's half my plan done now! I've got back to my right size. The next thing is, to get into that beautiful garden—how *is* that to be done, I wonder?"

And how was it to be done? There were signs pointing hither and yon, this way and that, but no signs pointing to the garden.

"If one only knew the right way—" said Alice to herself, and then she stopped, a little startled by seeing a Cheshire Cat sitting on a bough of a tree a few yards off.

The Cat grinned when it saw Alice. It looked good-natured, she thought. Still it had *very* long claws and a great many teeth, so she felt it ought to be treated with respect.

"Cheshire Puss," she began, rather timidly. She did not at all know whether it would like the name. However, it only grinned a little wider. "Come, it's pleased so far," thought Alice, and she went on. "Would you tell me, please, which way I ought to go from here?"

"That depends a good deal on where you want to get to," said the Cat. "In *that* direction lives a Hatter." The Cat waved its paw around. "And in *that* direction lives a March Hare. Visit either you like; they're both mad."

"But I don't want to go among mad people," Alice remarked.

"Oh, you can't help that," said the Cat. "We're all mad here. I'm mad. You're mad."

"How do you know I'm mad?" said Alice.

"You must be," said the Cat, "or you

wouldn't have come here. Are you going to play croquet with the Queen today?"

"I should like it very much," said Alice, "but I haven't been invited."

"You'll see me there," said the Cat, and it vanished.

Alice was not much surprised at this. She was well used to queer things happening. She waited a little, half expecting to see the Cat again, but it did not appear, and after a minute or two she walked on in the direction in which the March Hare was said to live. "I've seen hatters before," she said to herself. "The March Hare will be much the most interesting, and perhaps, as this is May, it won't be raving mad—at least not so mad as it was in March."

Soon she came in sight of the house of the March Hare. She thought it must be the right house because the chimneys were shaped like ears and the roof was thatched with fur.

There was a table set out under a tree in front of the house, and the March Hare and the Hatter were having tea at it. A Dormouse was sitting between them, fast asleep, and the other two were using it as

a cushion, resting their elbows on it, and talking over its head. "Very uncomfortable for the Dormouse," thought Alice, "only as it's asleep, I suppose it doesn't mind."

The table was a large one, but the three were all crowded together at one corner of it. "No room! No room!" they cried out when they saw Alice. "There's plenty of room!" said Alice indignantly, and she sat down in a large armchair at one end of the table.

"It isn't very civil of you to sit down without being invited," said the March Hare.

"I didn't know it was *your* table," said Alice. "It's laid for a great many more than three."

The party sat silent for a moment, and then the Hatter spoke. "What day of the month is it?" he asked Alice. He had taken his watch out of his pocket and was looking at it uneasily, shaking it every now and then, and holding it to his ear.

Alice considered a little, and then said, "The fourth."

"Two days wrong!" sighed the Hatter. "I told you butter wouldn't suit the works!" he added, looking angrily at the March Hare.

"It was the *best* butter," the March Hare meekly replied.

"Yes, but some crumbs must have got in as well," the Hatter grumbled. "You shouldn't have put it in with the bread knife."

The March Hare took the watch and looked at it gloomily. Then he dipped it into his cup of tea, and looked at it again.

"What a funny watch!" Alice remarked. "It tells the day of the month, and doesn't tell what o'clock it is!"

"Why should it?" muttered the Hatter. "Does *your* watch tell you what year it is?"

"Of course not," Alice replied very readily, "but that's because it stays the same year for such a long time together."

"Which is just the case with *mine*," said the Hatter.

Alice felt dreadfully puzzled. The Hatter's remark seemed to her to have no sort of meaning in it, and yet it was certainly English.

"I don't know what you mean," said Alice.

"Of course you don't!" the Hatter said, tossing his head contemptuously. "I dare say you never even spoke to Time!"

"Perhaps not," Alice cautiously replied, "but I know I have to beat time when I learn music."

"Ah!" said the Hatter. "He won't stand beating. Now, if you only kept on good terms with him, he'd do almost anything you liked with the clock. For instance, suppose it were nine o'clock in the morning, just time to begin lessons: you'd only have to whisper a hint to Time, and round goes the clock in a twinkling! Half-past one, time for dinner!"

("I only wish it was," the March Hare said to itself in a whisper.)

"That would be grand, certainly," said Alice, "but I shouldn't be hungry for dinner then, you know."

"Not at first, perhaps," said the Hatter, "but you could keep it to half-past one as long as you liked."

"Is that the way *you* manage?" Alice asked.

The Hatter shook his head mournfully. "Not I!" he replied. "We quarreled last March, at the great concert given by the Queen of Hearts. I had to sing:

'*Twinkle, twinkle, little bat!*
How I wonder where you're at!'
You know the song perhaps?"

"I've heard something like it," said Alice.

"It goes on, you know," the Hatter continued, "In this way:
'*Up above the world you fly,*
Like a tea-tray in the sky.'

"Well, I'd hardly finished the first verse when the Queen bawled out, 'He's murdering the time! Off with his head!'

"And ever since that," the Hatter went

on in a mournful tone, "he won't do a thing I ask. It's always six o'clock now."

A bright idea came into Alice's head. "Is that the reason so many tea things are put out here?" she asked.

"Yes, that's it," said the Hatter with a sigh. "It's always tea time, and we've no time to wash the things between whiles."

"Then you keep moving round, I suppose?" said Alice.

"Exactly so," said the Hatter, "as the things get used up."

"But what happens when you come to the beginning again?" Alice ventured to ask.

"Suppose we change the subject," the March Hare interrupted, yawning.

"I want a clean cup," said the Hatter. "Let's all move one place on."

He moved on as he spoke, and the sleepy Dormouse followed him. The March Hare moved into the Dormouse's place, and Alice rather unwillingly took the place of the March Hare. The Hatter was the only one who got any advantage from the change, and Alice was a good deal worse off than before, as the March Hare had just upset the milk jug into his plate.

"Really, now," said Alice, "I don't think—"

"Then you shouldn't talk," said the Hatter. He and the March Hare were attempting to put the Dormouse into the teapot.

Alice got up in great disgust and walked off. "I'll never go *there* again!" said Alice, as she picked her way through the wood. "It's the stupidest tea party I ever was at in all my life!"

Just as she said this, she noticed that one of the trees had a door leading right into it. "That's very curious!" she thought. "But everything's curious today. I think I may as well go in at once." And in she went.

Once more she found herself in the long hall, and close to the little glass table. "Now, I'll manage better this time," she said to herself, and began by taking the little golden key, and unlocking the door that led into the garden. Then she set to work nibbling at the mushroom (she had kept a piece of it in her pocket) till she was about a foot high. Then she went through the door and walked down the little passage, and *then* she found herself at last in the beautiful garden, among the bright flower beds and the cool fountains.

A large rose tree stood near the entrance of the garden. The roses growing on it were white, but the gardeners were busily painting them red. Alice thought this a very curious thing, and she went nearer to watch them, and, just as she came up to them, she heard one of them say, "Look out now, Two! Don't go splashing paint over me like that!"

"I couldn't help it," said Two, in a sulky tone. "Nine jogged my elbow."

On which Nine looked up and said, "That's right, Two! Always lay the blame on others!"

"*You'd* better not talk!" said Two. "I heard the Queen say only yesterday you deserved to be beheaded."

"What for?" said the one who had spoken first.

"That's none of your business, Seven!" said Nine.

"Yes, it *is* his business!" said Two. "And I'll tell him—it was for bringing the cook tulip roots instead of onions."

Nine flung down his brush, and had just begun, "Well, of all the unjust things—" when his eye chanced to fall upon Alice, and he checked himself suddenly. The others looked round also, and all of them bowed low.

"Would you tell me, please," said Alice, a little timidly, "why you are painting those roses?"

Seven and Nine looked at Two. Two began, in a low voice, "Why, the fact is, you see, Miss, this here ought to have been a *red* rose tree, and we put a white one in by mistake. If the Queen was to find it out, we should all have our heads cut off, you know. So you see, Miss, we're doing our best, afore she comes, to—"

At this moment, Five, who had been anxiously looking across the garden, called out, "The Queen! The Queen!" and the three gardeners instantly threw themselves flat upon their faces. There was a sound of many footsteps, and Alice looked around, eager to see the Queen.

Along came the Royal Procession. There were soldiers carrying clubs. Courtiers ornamented all over with diamonds walked two and two, as the soldiers did. After these came the royal children: there were ten of them, and the little dears came jumping merrily along, hand in hand, in couples. They were all ornamented with hearts. Next came the guests, mostly Kings and Queens. They were followed by the Knave of Hearts, carrying a crimson velvet cushion. Alice recognized the White Rabbit, who was next in line. He was blowing on a long trumpet and went by without noticing her.

Last of all in this grand procession came THE KING AND THE QUEEN OF HEARTS.

Alice was rather doubtful whether she ought not to lie down on her face like the three gardeners, but she could not remember ever having heard of such a rule at processions. "And besides, what would be the use

of a procession," thought she, "if people had all to lie down on their faces, so that they couldn't see it?" So she stood where she was, and waited.

When the procession came opposite to Alice, they all stopped and looked at her. "What's your name, child?" asked the Queen.

"My name is Alice, so please your Majesty," said Alice very politely. But she added to herself, "Why, they're only a pack of cards!"

"And who are *these*?" said the Queen, pointing to the three gardeners who were lying round the rose tree. As they were lying on their faces, and the pattern on their backs was the same as the rest of the pack, she could not tell whether they were gardeners, or soldiers, or courtiers, or several of her own children.

The Queen said to the Knave, "Turn them over!"

The Knave did so, very carefully, with one foot.

"Get up!" said the Queen, in a shrill loud voice, and the three gardeners instantly jumped up, and began bowing to the King, the Queen, the royal children, and everybody else.

"Leave off that!" screamed the Queen. "You make me giddy." And then, turning to the rose tree, she went on, "What have you been doing here?"

"May it please your Majesty," said Two, "we were trying—"

"I see!" said the Queen, who had meanwhile been examining the roses. "Off with their heads!" The procession moved on, three of the soldiers remaining behind to execute the unfortunate gardeners, who ran to Alice for protection.

"You shan't be beheaded!" said Alice, and she put them into a large flowerpot that stood near. The three soldiers wandered about for a minute or two, looking for them, and then quietly marched off after the others.

"Are their heads off?" shouted the Queen.

"Their heads are gone, if it please your Majesty!" the soldiers shouted in reply.

"That's right!" shouted the Queen. "Can you play croquet?"

The soldiers were silent, and looked at Alice, as the question was evidently meant for her.

"Yes!" shouted Alice.

"Come on, then!" roared the Queen, and Alice joined the procession, wondering very much what would happen next.

"Get to your places!" shouted the Queen in a voice of thunder, and people began running about in all directions, tumbling up against each other. However, they got settled down in a minute or two, and the game began.

Alice thought she had never seen such a curious croquet ground in her life. It was all ridges and furrows. The croquet balls were live hedgehogs, and the mallets live flamingoes, and the soldiers had to double themselves up and stand on their hands and feet to make the arches.

The players all played at once, without waiting for turns, quarreling all the while, and fighting for the hedgehogs. In a very short time the Queen was in a furious temper, and went stamping about and shouting, "Off with his head!" or "Off with her head!" about once in a minute.

Alice began to feel very uneasy. To be sure, she had not as yet had any dispute with the Queen, but she knew that it might happen any minute. "And then," thought she, "what would become of me? They're dreadfully fond of beheading people here. The great wonder is, that there's anyone left alive!"

She was looking about for some way of escape, and wondering whether she could get away without being seen, when she noticed a curious appearance in the air. It puzzled her very much at first, but after watching it a minute or two she made it out to be a grin, and she said to herself, "It's the Cheshire Cat. Now I shall have somebody to talk to!"

"How are you getting on?" said the Cat, as soon as there was mouth enough for it to speak with.

"I'd rather not," the Cat remarked.

"Don't be impertinent," said the King, "and don't look at me like that!" He got behind Alice as he spoke.

"A cat may look at a king," said Alice. "I've read that in some book, but I don't remember where."

"Well, it must be removed," said the King very decidedly, and he called to the Queen, who was passing at the moment, "My dear! I wish you would have this cat removed!"

The Queen had only one way of settling all difficulties, great or small. "Off with his head!" she said, without even looking round.

"I'll fetch the executioner myself," said the King eagerly, and he hurried off.

But when the executioner came, quite a dispute arose between him, the King, and the Queen. The executioner argued that you couldn't cut off a head unless there was a body to cut it off from; that he had never had to do such a thing before, and he wasn't going to begin at *his* time of life.

The King's argument was that anything that had a head could be beheaded, and that you weren't to talk nonsense.

The Queen's argument was that if something wasn't done about it in less than no time, she'd have everybody executed all round. This last remark made the whole party look grave and anxious.

The Cat's head began fading away, and soon it was entirely gone. The King and the executioner ran wildly up and down, looking for it.

"Let's go on with the game," the Queen said to Alice.

Alice did not say a word, but she did not want to go back to the game. Away she ran, through a maze of hedges.

"Off with her head!" the Queen shouted at the top of her voice.

An army of cards started after her.

"Off with her head! Off with her head!" screamed the Queen again. "Don't let her get away."

Alice turned toward the cardboard soldiers.

Alice waited till the eyes appeared, and then nodded. "It's no use speaking to it," she thought, "till its ears have come, or at least one of them." In another minute the whole head appeared, and then Alice put down her flamingo, and began an account of the game, feeling very glad she had someone to listen to her. The Cat seemed to think that there was enough of it now in sight, and no more of it appeared.

"How do you like the Queen?" said the Cat at last, in a low voice.

"Not at all," said Alice.

"Who *are* you talking to?" said the King, coming up to Alice, and looking at the Cat's head with great curiosity.

"It's a friend of mine—a Cheshire Cat," said Alice. "Allow me to introduce it."

"I don't like the look of it at all," said the King. "However, it may kiss my hand, if it likes."

164

"Who cares for *you*?" said Alice. "You're nothing but a pack of cards!"

At this the whole pack rose up into the air and came flying down upon her. She gave a little scream, half of fright and half of anger, and tried to beat them off, and found herself back on the river bank.

"Wake up, Alice dear!" said her sister. "Why, what a long sleep you've had!"

"Oh, I've had such a curious dream!" said Alice. And she told her sister of the strange adventure that you have just been reading about. And, when she had finished, her sister kissed her and said, "It *was* a curious dream, dear, certainly, but now run in to your tea. It's getting late."

So Alice got up and ran off, thinking while she ran, as well she might, what a wonderful dream it had been.

"But I'm just as glad," said Alice, "to be back where things are really what they seem."

Little Hiawatha
Indian Brave

Many years ago, when the forests were young, there lived a boy and his name was Hiawatha. He lived with his grandmother, whose name was Nokomis. His home was a tepee and it stood on the shore of a big, shining lake.

Nokomis was wise in the secrets of the forest, wise in the stories and legends the Indians told nightly around their campfires. She often told her grandson about them as he sat watching her weaving their warm woolen blankets, or grinding kernels of corn to use for their evening meal.

The small boy felt a thrill of pride at the stories. How he yearned to become a mighty hunter.

"You must learn the life of the forest," said Nokomis, and she explained a thousand and one things that were a question in the little lad's mind. What made the rainbow? What did the owls say when they hooted during the night? Why did the dogs bay at the moon? Why and where did the bears disappear during the cold winter months? Why? Why?

Each day the boy Hiawatha grew wiser in the secrets of the forest. He learned the language of the birds, how and where they built their nests. They were all friendly. He learned about the four-footed animals—the busy beavers, the squirrels, the soft-eyed deer, the rabbits. They were trusting friends, too.

One day the old arrow-maker fashioned a bow and arrow for Hiawatha and gave it to him as a gift. It was a small bow and a small arrow, for he was only a small boy. But Hiawatha felt as big and grown-up as any of the big and grown-up hunters.

"Now that I have a bow and arrow, I'll be a hunter today," he said to his friends the birds and animals.

"Are you going to hunt us?" they asked.

"Oh, no indeed," replied Hiawatha.

There was a green island across the lake.

"That is where I will go hunting," said Hiawatha. He carried his birch-bark canoe down to the water's edge. He stepped in. The obliging animals gave it a little push and the morning breeze and rippling waves gently carried him over to the island.

The canoe touched the shore. Hiawatha stood up to take a look. The canoe tipped. He lost his balance. Oops! Hiawatha fell in with a splash!

The water was not deep because he was so close to the land. He only got a good wetting. Hiawatha waded ashore and pulled his canoe up onto the beach.

Many bright little eyes watched the boy. Many little animals were laughing to themselves as they saw Hiawatha shake the water off himself. Surely this newcomer was not to be feared. Especially if he didn't know enough to get out of a canoe without falling into the lake.

But Hiawatha thought differently. Today

was the day he was going to start being a mighty hunter. In fact, right now! He looked around sharply and there, within easy reach of his arrow, were many animals. They were all staring at him in friendly curiosity. There were squirrels, birds of many feathers, flat-tailed beavers, a deer, chipmunks, and rabbits with twinkly noses. And they did not look one bit scared. That would never do! At least they should look afraid of a mighty hunter. Hiawatha decided to teach them a lesson, to make them respect and fear a hunter who had the name of Hiawatha.

The little Indian boy raised his bow. He pulled back on the bowstring to shoot the arrow. He pointed it at them. Before he could send that arrow whizzing through the air, it slipped from his hand and it fell to the ground. The animals were all amused and watched from safe places as he picked it up and set it in place again. Hiawatha would not give up easily.

Because Grandmother Nokomis had taught her grandson so well about the forest folk, Hiawatha knew they were surely laughing at him, the would-be hunter. He did not like that one bit!

"I didn't practice enough with my bow and arrow," said Hiawatha. "But they should be scared of a hunter, anyway."

For a minute Hiawatha was unhappy. And then—he saw strange tracks on the ground.

Never had he seen anything like them. Not a sign of the soft pads of a paw and none of claw marks, either.

"Grandmother, what animal makes tracks like these?" Hiawatha asked, forgetting his grandmother was at home and he was on his first hunting trip, all by himself.

"This is funnier and funnier," laughed the delighted animals. "We know whose prints those are, but we won't tell. Let him find out for himself."

The excited Indian boy studied the odd tracks again. "I will stalk this strange animal as a mighty hunter should do."

He put his ear to the ground, but he heard no thumping sound. On his hands and knees he followed the winding trail until suddenly he heard a sharp, whirring noise.

And there before him, in the middle of the path, stood a giant cricket, rubbing its wings together to make the sound the boy had heard.

Hiawatha stared into the big cricket's eyes, that stared back into his own. He forgot all about using his trusty bow. All he wanted to do was get away as fast as he could. He turned and fled.

The little forest animals thought it was the funniest thing they had ever seen. They popped out in the open and chirped and chattered and chuckled and chortled gleefully.

"Imagine! Afraid of a cricket!"

"And him with a bow and arrow, too!"

Hiawatha heard the taunts and teasing remarks and he knew they were poking fun

at him again. Instead of being brave, it looked as if he were a coward.

"Even we cottontails are not afraid of a cricket," said the littlest rabbit. He laughed so hard he could hardly sit up.

That brought Hiawatha to his senses in a hurry. He was angry at himself for running. He was embarrassed by their teasing. He was not acting like a brave hunter; he was acting like a scared boy. But he did not enjoy being laughed at—especially by anything so little as this little rabbit.

"I'll teach you not to laugh at me," cried Hiawatha. He grabbed his bow and arrow and pointed it straight at the heart of the littlest rabbit, who had laughed so hard at him.

The little rabbit took one look at Hiawatha's grim face. This was serious. He hopped, skipped, and jumped off as fast as he could. Around the bushes, between the trees, over the rocks, this frightened rabbit ran.

Panting, out of breath, the little rabbit at last had to give up. He could run no more. Hiawatha had cornered him and there was no escape.

The other animals all watched in horror as the Indian boy chased their friend. They gasped in dismay when the little rabbit reached the end of the trail and could go no more. They saw how the rabbit trembled in terror when Hiawatha pulled the bowstring taut, ready to shoot the arrow. It was a terrifying sight and there wasn't a thing they could do. What would that fellow do next?

A big tear rolled down the cheek of the frightened rabbit. If only he hadn't made such unkind remarks, if he had not laughed so long and so hard, this awful thing would not be happening.

Hiawatha saw the big tear. What was a mighty hunter to do? He could not shoot a poor little rabbit like that. After all, it *was* funny for anybody to be afraid of a cricket, especially a brave hunter. He should have taken it as a joke and laughed with the rest of the animals. But no, he had to get cross!

"I—I'm sorry," whimpered the rabbit.

"Aw!" said Hiawatha. "Scoot! Scat! Be off with you. I can't shoot you, I haven't the heart to do it."

The other animals were delighted to see that the little rabbit was safe and rushed out from their hiding places to thank the Indian boy. Hiawatha looked around in surprise. He saw their friendly faces and he saw they trusted him.

"I'll never hunt you again," declared Hiawatha firmly. "I like you, too." And to prove it, he broke his arrow and bow over his knees. There would be no more of hunting on this island.

Now that they were friends, they romped and played together happily.

A thought came into Hiawatha's mind. He realized that since he wasn't going to hunt,

he should do something else that was special —or what would he tell his grandmother?

"Let me see," said Hiawatha. "Hmmm—" He was puzzled what to do.

"Look around the island," suggested the birds. "It is very pretty from above."

"I can't fly, so I will have to see it from the ground," said Hiawatha.

"The brooks are cool and blue. We like them," said the beavers.

"The trees are green with leaves all summer long," said the raccoon.

"The bushes have lots of berries that are tasty to eat," said the chipmunks.

"In autumn there are lots of nuts. We

173

gather them for winter," said the squirrels.

"Sounds good," said Hiawatha. "I will be an explorer! I will find out what and who lives here. Then I will have something interesting to tell Grandmother."

The first thing for an explorer to do is to look for trails, of course. Oh, oh! Around the bend, in the middle of the path were paw marks so big that Hiawatha could hardly believe his eyes. He stepped into the first print with one foot, then with two feet— why, every paw print was so large they would hold both of his feet! There were long, sharp

claw marks besides. This was indeed a time for caution.

Not a sound broke the stillness except that twig he accidentally stepped on, and those stones that rolled off the path making a tinkling sound. Hiawatha crept along on his hands and knees. He approached a big round rock. The paw marks led around it. What was on the other side of the rock? He, Hiawatha, would find out!

174

But someone else, on the other side of the rock, heard that breaking twig and the sound of those rolling stones. He, too, wanted to find out what was approaching so stealthily.

didn't know what a boy was. He only saw that this creature was something down on all fours, like an animal. But it also had a feather, so it was like a bird, too.

Suddenly there they were, face to face, a frightened Hiawatha and a terrified bear cub. Hiawatha had often played with bear cubs, so he lost his fear immediately. This was a cute little fellow!

The bear cub had never seen a boy. He

One quick look was enough for the bear cub. He squealed in fear and dashed away as fast as his fat little legs would carry him. He glanced back over his shoulder and saw that this strange thing was coming after him, and now it was running on only two legs.

What's more, it was yelling at him. The cub didn't wait to listen. This was even more scary, if possible.

"Wait, wait," Hiawatha shouted to the cub. "Do not be afraid. I only want you to stay and play with us. Wait—wait," he puffed, "let me talk to you."

But the little cub headed for home and disappeared into the cave where he lived.

Hiawatha reached the bear cave. Something moved inside. Hiawatha jumped into the dark shadow, grabbing what he thought was the cub bear. "I caught you!" laughed Hiawatha and he held on tightly.

An angry, terrible roar almost burst his eardrums. A hot breath hit his face. He looked into a great mouth full of sharp teeth. This wasn't the cute bear cub he'd wanted to play with. This was the cub's very angry mother and he had grabbed her by the nose. Nothing could be worse!

The mama bear was furious at the stranger who had frightened her child. She did not know Hiawatha only wanted to play and that he meant no harm. Besides, her nose hurt when he grabbed it.

Hiawatha ran as he had never run before, but the huge mama bear with her lengthy, pounding strides, gained ground at every step. She roared so loud that it could be

heard all through the forest. Hiawatha was in deep, deep trouble—and all of his friends knew it.

The beavers sounded the first alarm by beating out the signal with their flat tails. The other animals heard it and ran to their secret meeting place. A chipmunk and squirrel were told to lead Hiawatha to the hidden clearing. The others knew what to do to help their friend, and they would have everything ready—if the bear did not catch Hiawatha first.

Meanwhile, the fleeing Hiawatha saw a tree on the other side of a small stream. Maybe that would be safe. He crossed the stream quickly. The bear did not fear the water and splashed through it, too. The old tree had lost some of its leaves and most of its limbs. The chipmunk and squirrel sat near the top, to observe the chase. The boy climbed almost to the top. The tree creaked with his weight, but he felt safe.

Not for long! Bears are good at tree-climbing, so up crawled the bear, as fast as she could. Two beavers came a-running and with their sharp teeth gnawed at the tree.

As the bear reached out to grab Hiawatha, the old tree swayed with her extra weight. Then, weakened at the base by the two beavers who were gnawing frantically at the trunk, the old tree gave one deep shudder and toppled over—CRASH!

Down came the bear, the breath knocked out of her. Down came Hiawatha. But the squirrel helped the boy as he fell, so he landed on the ground gently.

"Follow us," said the squirrel.

"Hurry, hurry," said the chipmunk.

Hiawatha had to run away before the bear got back her breath and resumed the chase. The squirrel and the chipmunk were to guide him to the clearing.

From the moment the beavers had sounded the alarm, the other animals had been very busy. They dragged two fallen branches to be used as outer shafts for a simple cart. The raccoons and chipmunks found something that would serve as reins and a harness. They tied a crosspiece between the shafts for a footboard. The fawn, who could run almost as fast as the wind—and that is faster than a bear can run—stepped inside the harness. All was ready when the squirrel guided Hiawatha to the clearing.

"Here! Get on this! Take these reins." All the animals joined in showing him what to do. Hiawatha obeyed gladly.

"Giddap!" they shouted. "Now get going!"

They could hear the big bear's roar getting closer and closer, closer and closer.

The fawn leaped ahead and in a flash Hiawatha was whizzing over the ground in the fastest ride he would ever have in his whole life. The forest closed in around the fleeing pair. The fawn and the small forest friends knew many shorter paths, and all the safe hidden trails, and these were the paths they used.

The other small animals had a hard time keeping up with the speedy deer. Some of them had to leap from tree to tree—and some had to hop, skip, and jump. But they were all determined to be on hand to say good-bye to their friend.

The roars and growls of the bear seemed more faint. At last they were only a whisper of sound and then they faded out completely. The bear was left far behind.

Hiawatha realized that now he was safe from the bear, but he still had to cross the lake to get home. The afternoon sun was sinking low in the sky as Hiawatha and his helpful friends arrived at the lake shore.

"Thanks, everybody," said Hiawatha. "I will never forget all you have done for me. I'll go home in my canoe and I will always remember you."

His canoe? Hiawatha looked where his canoe had been beached.

"My canoe! It's gone!" cried Hiawatha.

The animals pointed toward the middle of the lake. There was the canoe, drifting out.

Hiawatha almost wept. "I didn't pull it up far enough, and I can't swim to get it. Without my canoe I can't go home."

"Don't worry, we will get your canoe,"

said the beavers. "We are good swimmers."

They dived gracefully in the water, swam out to the canoe, and pushed it easily to shore. They held it steady as Hiawatha, using the turtle as a stepping-stone, got inside and settled down. And there he sat!

"Where is your paddle?" asked a beaver.

"Did you lose that, too?" asked another.

"Yes, I guess so," said Hiawatha, "but I didn't use it. The breeze brought me."

"Well, there's no breeze now," said the beavers, "and we may not have one for an hour, and maybe not until morning."

"Oh my, how will I get home?" the boy asked anxiously.

The two beavers whispered slyly to each other and passed the word along. All the animals nodded their heads in agreement.

"We will be glad to help you if you'll promise us something," said the beavers.

"Oh, I will," said Hiawatha. "But what should I promise?"

"That you will come again soon."

"I will," said Hiawatha gladly.

The beavers turned the bow of the canoe homeward, and using their flat tails as the paddles, they skimmed the canoe across the shining water, to Hiawatha's tepee. Then

they bade him a fond good-bye and swam back to their island.

It was almost dark when Hiawatha arrived home. The sun was setting in the west and the stars were beginning to twinkle above.

Grandmother Nokomis was waiting at the tepee for him. She had his supper ready.

Hiawatha did not realize how hungry he really was until he saw all the good things his grandmother had prepared. He ate very quickly. He looked into the fire and yawned.

"Today I was a mighty Hiawatha and so I hunted, but—" his voice drifted off.

"Ah, but now—" Grandmother Nokomis gathered a nodding child in her arms. "But now," she repeated with a loving smile, "now you are a mighty *little* Hiawatha, sound asleep."

And Hiawatha, mighty little Hiawatha, dreamed happily the whole night long.

Casey Jones
Railroad Man

C*asey Jones* fell in love with railroading when he was just a boy. Maybe it was while he was lying on a little rise of land beyond the cornfields, watching locomotives chug past. Maybe it was while he lay wakeful in the summer nights, listening to the sweet-sad sound of the train whistles. However it came about, when Casey was thirteen years old, he knew what he wanted to do. He wanted to be a locomotive engineer—the bravest, best railroad engineer ever to get a train through on time.

'Course Casey had some growing to attend to first, and he set about it with a right goodwill. Casey did so well that by the time he was old enough to be an engineer, he was so tall he couldn't stand up in an engine cab without sticking his head out the window.

Casey had a beautiful engine, and he took care of it the way a mother cat watches out for her kittens. Casey's engine was cleaned and it was oiled and it was polished till it shone, or Casey knew the reason why. And if it needed fixing, Casey went right along into the shop with it and saw that it got fixed, and fixed right.

Casey had a special calliope whistle for his engine, and that whistle had six tones. He could just about play a tune with it, and all the flagmen up and down the tracks knew by the sound of it when the train passing had Casey Jones at the throttle.

So Casey went on railroading, and playing his calliope whistle, and getting his trains through on time, and he got kind of famous among railroad folk. For one thing, they just plain liked him. He was a pleasant man to work with. For another, though he might

183

take a few chances now and then, he'd never lost a passenger or a crewman in an accident. Casey was mighty proud of that record.

Then, one cloudy, nasty, rainy night, Casey was called to take a "Cannonball." That's the name for a fast train, and a fast train was the kind Casey liked best. Only this particular train was over an hour late in starting out of the station.

Well, Casey didn't let that discourage him. He knew every inch of the track ahead of him better than most men know their own front parlors. And he sure knew how to make up time.

So off Casey went, screeching along the rails at seventy miles an hour. Some say that with Casey at the throttle, and that throttle full open, the train was doing better than seventy. They whizzed along through that murky night, past sleeping villages, and Casey's calliope whistle sang out again and again.

Then, all of a sudden, there was a sound like a big firecracker, and it came from right under the wheels of Casey's locomotive. Casey's fireman heard it. He knew what it meant, and so did Casey. It was a signal. They called it a torpedo, and a flagman had

put it on the track. There was something wrong up ahead.

The fireman jumped to look out of that cab, and what he saw ahead was enough to make any man's heart leap clean up between his ears. There, just a few hundred yards down the track, was another train.

"Jump for your life!" yelled the fireman.

"You jump!" Casey yelled back. "I'll stay!"

Casey grabbed the brake and the train began to slow. The fireman jumped. And Casey? Casey Jones stayed, with one hand on the throttle and the other on the brake. That's the way they found him when they pried into the wreckage of his engine. He'd stayed, and because he'd stayed, Casey slowed that thundering Cannonball down and kept his record clear. He never did lose a crewman or a passenger. He'd lost his own life, but the men who knew him best figured he'd rather have it that way.

Lots of men are heroes, but not all heroes become legends. Sometimes it takes a song to make a legend, and before long the railroaders were singing about the brave engineer. The Ballad of Casey Jones is still sung today. There are lots of different versions, and most of them go something like this:

Put in your water and shovel in your coal,
Put your head out the window, watch the
    drivers roll,
I'll run her open till she leaves the rail,
'Cause we're eight hours late with the
    Western Mail!
He looked at his watch and his watch was
    slow,
Looked at the water and the water was low,
Turned to his fireboy and then he said,
"We'll get to 'Frisco, but we'll all be dead!"

Casey Jones, he mounted to the cabin,
Casey Jones, with his orders in his hand!
Casey Jones, he mounted to the cabin,
Took his farewell trip into the promised land.

Come all you rounders if you want to hear
The story of a brave engineer;
Casey Jones was the hogger's name,
On a big eight-wheeler, boys, he won his
    fame.
Caller called Casey at half-past four,
He kissed his wife at the station door,
Mounted to the cabin with orders in his hand
And took his farewell trip to the promised
    land.

Casey Jones, he mounted to the cabin,
Casey Jones, with his orders in his hand!
Casey Jones, he mounted to the cabin,
Took his farewell trip into the promised land.

Casey pulled up old Reno Hill,
Tooted for the crossing with an awful shrill,
The switchmen knew by the whistle's moans
That the man at the throttle was Casey Jones.
He pulled up short two miles from the place,
Number Four stared him right in the face,
Turned to his fireboy, said, "You'd better
    jump,
'Cause there's two locomotives that're going
    to bump!"

Fireman jumped, but Casey stayed on.
He was a good engineer, but he's dead and
    gone.
Casey Jones, stayed inside his cabin,
Took his farewell trip into the promised land.

Pecos Bill
Great Cowboy

Down Texas way a river flows. Where it comes from no one knows. Where it is going to no one cares, so long as it runs away from there! It is the Pecos River. It was down in the valley of that river that Pecos Bill made his home.

The story of Pecos Bill began this way: A covered wagon was crossing the Texas plains. Lots of wagons were in those days. Everyone was looking for more room out in the wide West.

The family in this wagon really needed elbow room. The wagon was filled to the top with big boys and small ones, little girls and tall ones. There were pots and pans and jars and crocks and churns. That wagon was full! It was noisy, too, what with children talking and laughing and crying, all at the same time. So perhaps it isn't surprising that no one noticed when the smallest boy of all, a baby named Bill, rolled off the back of the wagon and went bouncing away . . .

The wagon rolled on, and there sat the baby, baby Bill, all alone on the Texas plain. Well, he wasn't really alone. There were animals aplenty. When one coyote pup came sniffing along, Bill followed that pup, and by nightfall they reached a coyote den.

When the mother coyote came home, it was quite a surprise for her to find that a strange little critter had jointed her litter! She could soon see he was tough and a match for any pup. He could out-scrap and out-howl all the rest right off, so the mother coyote made him feel at home. And that's where Bill grew up.

Soon he knew every trick the coyotes knew, and he learned a thing or two from other animals as well. He had hardly cut his baby teeth before he could out-hiss any snake. By the time he was three he could out-jump a jack rabbit. Before he was four he could outrun a deer.

When Bill was seven or nine or thereabouts —no one was keeping much track—a stranger appeared in Pecos Land. It was a baby horse. That little colt was all alone and about tuckered out. A pack of vultures was wheeling around, circling lower and lower overhead, just waiting for the end.

Then Bill appeared, young Pecos Bill. He sailed into those vultures and set their feathers flying. He found the poor colt some water. He took him home and gave him some food.

From that time on, if you saw Pecos Bill you were sure to see the horse. Those two were always together, close as warts on a toad. Not that they always agreed. When the

time came for the horse to be broken to saddle, they had one big disagreement. Seemed the horse plumb didn't want a saddle on his back. He didn't want to be ridden. Matter of fact, he was tough about it. Only thing was, Pecos Bill was tougher as that bronco soon discovered. Pecos was soon in the saddle to stay.

When word got around of the great bronco-buster, some cowboys there in the Texas country figured they were as tough as anyone around, and they could ride that mustang, too. So they tried. Kept a crew busy for quite a spell picking those cowboys up and carting them away after they'd taken their turns.

That's when Pecos Bill's horse got his name —Widowmaker.

And that's how Pecos Bill got his career— cowboy. He was the roughest, toughest cowboy west of the Alamo. Bill and his horse Widowmaker were known through all the West. That is to say, Bill and his horse— and his rope! For Bill could rope with his lariat anything he could see.

Bill said, "I could rope the lightning, or a drop of falling rain."

No one doubted him, least of all after the day the cyclone came. That day the Texas sky was dark. A howling, twisting cyclone was blowing out of nowhere down on the Texas plains. It was knocking the legs out from under horses. It was blowing away cows and barns. That cyclone was bad, all right, but what could anybody do to stop it? Somebody thought of Bill.

Pecos Bill was ready to try. He jumped on Widowmaker and they chased after that swift black cloud. Pecos lassoed the cyclone and it heaved and bucked and blew, but in vain. Bill tamed it to a breeze!

By this time Bill had got himself a herd of cattle. He was mighty proud of those cows. But a band of cow thieves came whooping down the Pecos Valley. They were rounding up prize beef. When Bill came down from that cyclone trip, he found that the thieves had made off with his whole herd.

Bill didn't like that. He didn't like it one bit. He and Widowmaker started out after the thieves, and caught up with them in the hills. What a beating Bill gave those fellows! He roped them and he shook them and he slapped them around. All the gold flew out of the bad men's teeth, folks say. That is why there is gold in those hills to this day.

Bill and Widowmaker started for home, driving Bill's whole herd. They had a mighty wide desert to cross, mile after mile of burning sand. First they ran out of grass for the cattle. Then Bill ran out of food. That was bad enough; but even worse, they all needed water. Even Bill's canteen was dry.

Bill knew he and his herd would never make it home if he couldn't find some water. He was really burned dry, and so were the poor cows. So Bill took a stick and he dug in the sand. He scraped till he dug the whole Rio Grande!

There is another time folks tell about. Some Indians were on the warpath. They got out their war paint, and they painted themselves up for battle from head to toe. They looked mighty wild and rough, and they felt it!

They built a big campfire and got out their drums, and they started up a wild war dance. "We heap big warriors, hoo hoo hoo!" they

chanted as they danced. What a hullabaloo! "Ugh!" they cried. "We tough guys! Each one tougher than two."

But they had forgotten Pecos Bill!

Bill heard about the Indians' plans. "I'll fix those Injuns," he said. And those who heard him saw his eyes begin to glow.

Bill and Widowmaker started out by night on the Indians' trail. They raised a blazing cloud of stardust behind them on the plain.

"Smoke signals!" cried the Indians. "Big trouble heading this way!" And they started to run.

Closer came the dust cloud under Widow-maker's pounding hoofs. Faster and faster the Indians ran. They ran right out of their war paint! Yessirree! Left it in bright streaks behind them on the desert's rocky walls. You can see it in Arizona to this day, there in the Painted Desert.

To celebrate, Pecos Bill threw a leg over a cloud and started shooting stars out of the sky. Bang, bang, bang! Down went star after star, till there was just one big bright one left in the sky.

Bill blew on his gun and put it back in his holster.

"I'll leave that star for Texas," he said.

And that is why Texas is known as the Lone Star State.

Seemed there was nothing Bill couldn't handle, until along came Sluefoot Sue. She came riding down the river on a giant fish. Fresh as the dew on a prairie rose was Sue. She was also the first woman Pecos Bill had seen.

When he looked at her, he felt a pounding in his ears and a churning in his chest. His blood was a-boiling and his stomach did flip-flops, so he knew this must be love.

This was agreeable to Sue, and they set a wedding day. But there was a price Bill had to pay.

"First," said Sue, "I want a bouncy bustle. It's the latest style these days."

That was fine with Bill. He made her one from a bunch of wire springs.

"Second," said Sue, batting her eyes of blue, "I want to ride Widowmaker."

Ride Widowmaker? That was not so easy. Bill was willing, but how about Widowmaker? He was a tough old one-man horse. Nothing had ever come between him and Bill. Would the first thing be sweet Sue?

Widowmaker tossed his head and he whin-nied and snorted. But at last Pecos Bill sweet-talked him into letting Sue jump into the saddle on his back.

Sue was pleased—but then, she didn't see the mean look in old Widowmaker's eye.

Well, away they went, Widowmaker and Sue. Everyone in the Pecos land was there to watch. And Widowmaker really gave them a show. He put on a one-horse rodeo. He kicked and he galloped. He snorted and he bucked. He rolled his mean old fiery eyes. But Sue stuck on.

She hung on as tight as a saddle burr—until her bustle began to bounce! *Sproing!* went those wire springs. Up went Sue! Down she came into the saddle again. *Sproing!* went the springs, and up again she flew.

Higher and higher and *higher* bounced Sue, up, up into the sky. There was just one chance to save her. That was Pecos Bill's lariat. He'd roped bears and flying buzzards, he had roped a railroad train. He had roped a whirling cyclone and a drop of falling rain. Surely he could lasso Sluefoot Sue!

Bill coiled his lariat. He swung the loop of rope. Sue bounced once more, and as she flew, he let the coil of rope fly, too.

No one spoke, no one breathed as the rope snaked upward after the soaring figure of Sue. Then the loop of the lariat quivered in

the air. Down it came. Pecos Bill had missed.

The crowd could not believe it. They were plumb baffled. But they hadn't looked at Widowmaker. They hadn't seen the mean look in his flashing old eyes as he stepped on the end of Bill's rope!

Sue sailed on up into the sky, out of sight behind a cloud. And she was never seen again.

That broke Bill's heart. He rode away across the plains and he never returned. Some say he went back to the coyotes. They say that when the coyotes howl at the moon when it is full, you can hear Pecos Bill howling with them. He is lonesome, they say, for Sluefoot Sue, still bouncing somewhere among the clouds.

That's not real certain, but one thing is sure: Ask who the greatest cowboy is and still everyone in Texas land will tell you, "Pecos Bill!"

194

Paul Bunyan
Giant of the Forest

In the great Northland the rivers run swift, and trees grow tall enough to blot out the sun. It takes big men to tame that timber and float the logs down through white water to the lumber mills.

Yes, lumbering men are a big, proud lot. But they take off their caps at the name of Paul Bunyan, the greatest logger of them all.

Where Paul was born is not quite clear. Some say he's a Downeaster from the State of Maine. They say his cradle was so big it was anchored in the ocean off the shore. It rocked up waves that tumbled in to make the highest tides ever seen.

When Paul learned to walk, he once tumbled down and flattened all the trees on the hill above his town—which may or may not have been Wiscasset, Maine.

It took the whole town to raise that child.

In one meal he drank all the milk a herd of cows could give in a week. And making his clothes kept the women sewing from dawn to dark.

The folks of that village kept on feeding and clothing and loving the boy until he became a fine, hungry giant of a man, sixty-three ax handles high. Then he saw that he was eating them out of house and home, so Paul went out West where there was lots of room.

Paul had no more than reached the Middle West when the Winter of the Blue Snow came howling down. Yessir, the snow was blue with cold that year.

One day as Paul was snowshoeing over the countryside, he saw a big blue drift shiver and shake. In the drift, he discovered a calf, turned blue from the cold.

That calf was no more than six feet high, so Paul thawed him out and named him Babe and took him home for a pet. But Babe grew two feet every time anyone looked at him! Soon he was quite some size—as big for an ox as Paul was for a man. That was going some! And he stayed bright blue.

When spring came, Paul and Babe wandered around the countryside looking for a job their size. Babe's hoofs sank into the soft spring ground as they went. The spring rains filled the hoofprints and made the lakes you see to this day out in Wisconsin and Minnesota.

Paul took another look around the countryside. "Trees!" he said to Babe. "That's what grows biggest in this ground. Trees are the crop for you and me. We'll set us up a lumber camp, Babe my friend!"

So they did. They set up a camp deep in the north woods. Paul melted down seventy-seven ax blades to make him one fifteen-foot, two-bladed ax. In one swing he could flatten all the trees on a four-acre plot. If he hap-

pened to miss a few on a swing, he'd pick them off as he pulled the ax back.

Paul moved around the country a lot, looking over timberland. It was rough country for travel in those days, but that was no trouble to Paul. He could cross big Lake Superior in three good jumps. The Mississippi he could jump across and back without touching.

When Paul needed a meal, he could always do some hunting. There were plenty of bear, deer, moose, and wolves around in those days though even Paul would admit that wolf meat didn't make much of a meal. When Paul was hunting, just for fun he liked to straighten out twisting animal trails. He'd fasten Babe's harness to one end and just pull away in a good straight line. You could hear the crunching back in the trees as that old trail straightened out. One of those trails makes the boundary line between the Dakotas today.

Babe was handy in other ways, too. When Paul and his crew got their first forest lumbered off, they found they had forgotten something. There was no river to float the logs down. They were a good long distance from a sawmill, and there were no roads between.

That didn't stop Paul for long. He hitched Babe to a plow and they dug them a river,

right over to the Mississippi, and the logs went floating down. The Missouri, folks call that stream Babe and Paul Bunyan dug.

The lumbermen got a great kick out of watching Paul and Babe at work. That was one reason loggers from east and west came looking for a chance to work in his camp. But there were other reasons why they liked Paul Bunyan's camp best of all.

Take Paul's cook shack; it was really big. He had horse-drawn teams to carry loads of food down the long rows of tables to get it to the men good and hot. There were boys on roller skates to pass salt and pepper and bread and butter in a hurry.

Out in the kitchen was the famous pancake griddle, bigger than a school gymnasium. Paul hired boys whose whole job was to keep that griddle greased. They skated all day on its red-hot top, wearing slabs of bacon strapped to their feet. The wise ones strapped extra slabs to the seat of their pants in case of a fall.

Once, for a treat, the cook popped popcorn on the griddle. Well, the corn popped up in such a blizzard that the cook boys were lost, twenty of them. It took them eight days to eat their way out of the great drifts of popcorn.

Some great meals were stirred up in Paul Bunyan's cook shack, all right. But they took a lot of planning, too. Paul logged off all the trees in North and South Dakota. Then with a shovel he flattened all the mountain tops, and he laid out farms to grow vegetables.

Of course there were some stumps left, but Paul pounded them down into the ground with a mallet, one blow to a stump. Soon the ground was as level as a table, all set for seeds. When the garden plots got dry, Paul would roll up some clouds wherever he found them and bring them back to give his fields a good soaking rain.

There were times, though, when even that garden didn't keep the camp in food. For example, there was the Year of the Two

Winters. Summer never did come. As soon as one winter was over, the next one began. It snowed and snowed.

The trees were covered with snow, so the men couldn't work. They hung around in the bunkhouses, singing and roughhousing. When they decided to get some shut-eye, they found the flames in the lanterns had frozen! Couldn't sleep with all those lantern lights, so they threw the flames out into the snow. Forgot all about 'em until spring came when those flames melted down and set the woods on fire. But that's another story. Back in the dead of winter the men still had to eat, and the camp ran out of food in that Year of Two Winters.

Paul set out with Babe the Blue Ox to see what he could find. All he found was a load of dried peas. Well, that was better than nothing. So Paul started to haul it back to camp.

He was nearly home when, as he crossed a frozen lake, the ice broke. In went the load of peas, wagon, and all!

That was bad, but it wasn't enough to stop Paul. He called his men from the camp nearby. They shoveled away the snow and cut down all the trees around the shore of that lake. They heaped up the logs and set them afire. Well, sir, they turned that whole lake into one big soup pot. They had a lake full of green pea soup.

They froze some on sticks, like lollipops, and took them to the woods for lunch as the snow began to melt. But by the end of the week they were sick of pea soup. By the time the snow was gone, that lumber crew never wanted to hear the words p— s— again.

It was the following spring when a strange thing happened. Paul set up camp on a river bank, and his men soon filled the river with

199

logs. When the time came for the big drive, crews started downriver with the rafts of logs. Day after day they floated down, with nothing but forests on the banks. After some days they spotted a lumber camp on the river bank. That was a welcome sight. They waved and shouted greetings. Then they rubbed their eyes and looked again.

It was their own camp they were drifting by! That river ran around in a circle; they were back where they had started from. You can hear men tell even today of that Round River drive.

They tell, too, of the dry spell in the Big Onion River country. That year no rain fell.

First the leaves dried up on all the trees. By the time Paul's crew got the timber cut and stacked for the drive, the river had dried up, too. Now that was bad. Just one spark could burn up their whole winter's work. And they couldn't sell timber stacked up in the woods.

So Paul and Babe set off again. They bought up the whole onion crop of Kansas and Nebraska. When they came back, Paul fed the men raw onions until every man was weeping a steady stream of tears right into the river bed. Soon that river was racing along again, and Paul and his men drove their logs down a river of onion tears.

Oh, those were the days, when the West was young and the logging camps were in full swing. But it didn't take long for crews like Paul's to slash through the forests. Farms began to grow up where towering trees had stood. Towns grew up among the farms. Soon the country was plumb settled; there wasn't room for Paul Bunyan.

Paul and Babe had worked their way west clear to the Pacific Coast. Now when the great Northwest went civilized too, with power saws buzzing in the woods, Paul and Babe turned their backs on it all and headed north.

Some say Paul has a camp near Hudson Bay. Some say he is logging Alaskan trees. Men who wander in the forests and listen to the breeze say that now and then they hear a deep voice singing far away:

Oh, everybody's heard of me,
The logging man, Paul Bunyan,
How me and Babe the Big Blue Ox
Made camp on the old Big Onion.
We cut trees on a mountain
That stood upon its head.
We straightened crooked rivers
To find out where they led. . . .

If you wander in the forest, just listen to the breeze. You may hear a deep voice far away, singing through the trees. See Northern Lights a-glimmering in curtains, fans, and wheels? That's Babe and old Paul Bunyan just kicking up their heels!

201

Windwagon Smith
Prairie Sailor

Back in the days when the West was young, there were scouts and explorers and fighting men who blazed trails into the wilds. Close behind them came the pioneers with their families, rolling by the wagonload out to the free lands to make themselves new homes.

No sooner did a pioneer get up the walls and roofs of a new home than his wife began thinking of things she wanted. She wanted salt for the salt box and flour for the flour barrel and a nice piece of side pork for the stew kettle. She also hankered for turkey-red curtains and fancy oil lamps, hair ribbons for the girls and knee patches for the boys, and a new bonnet for herself to wear to the nearest town.

So pretty soon there were traders on the trails, hauling goods to sell to the pioneers. The Oregon Trail and the Santa Fe Trail were the two that were known the best. It was on the trail to old Santa Fe down in Mexican Territory that this tale was spun.

Its proper beginning was up in Kansas in a little prairie town. That little town, Old Westport, mostly just drowsed in the dust under the Kansas sun. It only woke up when a wagon train was gathering for the long haul, nearly a thousand miles, down to Santa Fe. Then every man jack dreamed a dream of the riches to be made hauling freight to Santa Fe.

One day things were so quiet you could hear two little dust motes colliding in a sunbeam, if you opened your eyes to listen. The city fathers were sitting in a row on the porch of the Star of the West. This café was, so to speak, the social center of the town; and there sat the city fathers with their chairs tilted back and their feet on the porch rail, with their eyes shut, thinking deep thoughts.

"Ahoy there!" a voice bellowed, and every eye snapped open at once to gaze on a wondrous sight.

Drawn up in front of the Star of the West was a covered Conestoga wagon—but such a covered wagon as they'd never seen before. Like the usual ones, it was high as a house, with wheels as tall as a man. But this one had no teams of dusty oxen out in front. Instead, on top of the wagon a deck ran

from stem to stern, for all the world like a ship at sea. Aloft was a mast rigged with a tattered sail to catch the prairie wind. And at the rear—beg your pardon, the stern—a tiller swung a rudder.

"A gen-u-ine prairie schooner!" gasped one of the city fathers.

With a clang an anchor dropped over the side, landing neat as a horseshoe around a hitching post. And from the deck a voice like a foghorn called again, "Avast, me hearties!"

Down rattled every foot from the porch rail as the city fathers sprang to attention. Mayor Crum stepped forward.

"Howdy!" said the Mayor, after clearing his throat. "Stranger, where are you from?"

"Avast there, lubbers!" said the stranger. "My name is Captain Smith, and I come from the seven seas. Now I've built me this tidy schooner and cruised to the West to sail the lone prairies."

"Hmm," said the Mayor, thinking deep, "no oxen to feed, I see. As for your sails, we know there's wind enough in Kansas. Tell me, sir, can your craft haul freight?"

"You can bet your last blinking barnacle," cried Cap'n Smith. "Freight is ballast, you know. Her hold will take a full cargo. She'll sail the prairie as if it were the sea."

As he spoke, he slid down a rope to the street, and in less than the time it takes to say "Windwagon Smith's Conestoga Schooner," Cap'n Smith and the city fathers were gathered around a table in the Star of the West, deep in palaver.

"Now look at the course charted here on the map, the trail leads down to old Santa Fe," Cap'n Smith said to the Kansas folk. "Oxen and wagons take almost two months. I'll sail it in fourteen days."

The storekeeper was a sharp one for figuring things out, so he took pencil in hand with a pad. He scratched down some figures.

"That's a quarter of the time," he said. He wrote some more figures and pushed them about. "Why, that's four times the profit! Land sakes!"

"With a whole fleet of windwagons," the Mayor said dreamily, "look at the money we'd make!"

Captain Smith pulled out a thick wad of papers. The men gathered around. "Just so happens," smiled Smith, "that I have charts here with me for a super windwagon."

Well, before that meeting disbanded they had settled a thing or two.

"We'll name her the *Prairie Clipper!*" Mayor Crum soon decreed.

He and the others dipped into their wallets for money to pay for the keel. And they settled the bargain with handshakes over bowls of buffalo stew.

Now the waitress at the Star of the West was Molly, the Mayor's daughter. A beautiful girl was she, with hair like a Zanzibar sunset and eyes like the deep-blue sea. While the town leaders were busy adding up their profits in their heads, Captain Smith kept his eyes on Molly, adding up this and that, too.

There was no drowsing in Old Westport on sunny days from then on. Everyone was busy working on the clipper. They laid out the keel, with ribs of the stoutest hickory and white oak. They chose the sturdiest birch for the wheels. They sawed and they hammered and they planed.

But every night after work was done, Captain Smith and Molly climbed to the craft's highest perch. There they'd sit beneath the same moon that shines down on the seven seas, with buffalo grass billowing all around. And Captain Smith would tell her tales of life on the ocean deep.

Well, the keel was laid, the hull was caulked, the deck was holystoned, and the mast was raised. The Ladies Sewing Circle marched down Main Street to present the sail. And the *Prairie Clipper* was ready for launching.

What a sight for everyone's eyes! Her twelve-foot wheels rose from the grass tops. Her mast seemed to scrape the skies!

Up the gangplank marched all the investors. No one noticed that in the excitement sweet Molly had stowed away. Then the brass band played. Captain Smith raised the sail. He grabbed the long tiller as the sail billowed out in the Kansas breeze. And the windwagon started to roll!

What a cheer went up from the watching crowd as the *Prairie Clipper* headed down the Santa Fe trail, picking up speed like a song. The city fathers lined the rail, waving their hats with pride.

Out into the sea of buffalo grass the windship pointed her prow. The Captain hauled on the tiller pole to steer her this way around a hill where coyotes sang, that way around an Indian camp.

Faster and faster the windwagon rolled. She swayed and she rattled and bumped. One by one the city fathers left the rail and staggered down into the hold, where they groaned and they moaned as they were thumped about.

"Let us out!" cried the Mayor. "Put us ashore. Stop this contraption or we'll sue!"

"Right you are!" said the Captain. "Hold on tight and I'll bring her about."

He pushed on the tiller. The axles groaned. The windwagon laid over hard, tumbling the men in the hold. Then she swung in a half-circle, turning back toward town, with the sail angling out from the mast.

Captain Smith took a deep breath and pulled on the tiller to straighten her out on course. Doggone it, the wheels stuck fast!

Smith pulled and he tugged with all his might, but those wheels would not unjam! They cut a swath through the buffalo grass in a circle two miles wide.

Now each time the wagon circled near the town, a man or two would jump out. The townsfolk gathered to watch their neighbors return and to pick them up and dust them off.

When the men were all ashore, the wagon still sailed. The townsfolk could see Captain Smith on the deck. They could hear him cry as the wagon sailed by, "Farewell! I'll go down with the wreck!"

But what was this? Next time the wagon hove into sight, there was sweet Molly at the Captain's side. She had climbed from her hiding place in the hold to join Wind-wagon Smith at his lonely post.

"You'd better get off!" cried the Captain. "We're in for a blow from a hurricane. I'm afraid her seams will rip."

Sure enough, across the prairie loomed a mean-looking black cloud.

"We can ride it out, Captain!" sang Molly.

But just then the twister hit! As the windwagon sunfished and tilted and bucked, the tiller wrenched itself free.

"We *will* ride out the gale!" cried the Captain. "I can steer her again!"

He got a firm grip on the tiller, and away they sailed, straight as a string. But that twister spun down and picked up the windwagon. The last the townsfolk saw of it, the *Prairie Clipper* was sailing off on the top of the storm as the twister departed, due west.

That old windwagon was never seen again. But in tales the oldtimers told they spoke of a ship they saw in the clouds when the sunset had turned to gold. She'd be sailing across the painted sky, with Windwagon Smith at the tiller, and sweet Molly standing close by his side. They said you could hear Cap'n Smith a-singing high above:

> *Yippy-ay, we're sailing,*
> *A-sailing are we,*
> *Just Molly and I*
> *On the lone prairie*
> *In our wagon way up in the sky, the*
>   *sky,*
> *In our windwagon up in the sky.*

Uncle Remus Stories

Johnny and Uncle Remus were friends. Johnny's hair was brown, his skin was fair, and he was not quite nine. Uncle Remus' hair was white, his skin was black, and no one knew how old he was.

The reason Johnny loved Uncle Remus so much was the wonderful things that he knew. He knew everything there was to know about the birds, the animals, and all the creatures. He even understood the language they used when they spoke; he understood what the Screech-Owl said to the Hoot-Owl in the tree outside his cabin; he understood *I-doom-er-ker-kum-mer-ker*,

the Turtle talk, that bubbled up from the bottom of the creek.

Johnny liked to hear Uncle Remus tell stories about what the creatures were doing, and he liked the funny old-fashioned way he spoke. Every evening before supper, he and his friend Ginny went down to Uncle Remus' cabin to listen. All Uncle Remus had to do was to take one puff on his pipe, and a story would just start rolling out with the smoke. It might be a story about a Lion, an Elephant, or a Bullfrog; but most of the stories were about that smartest of all little creatures, Brer Rabbit—

I do believe it's time I told you about the folks who live down in the briar patch.

They aren't folks like you and me, but I'll be mighty pleased if you'll follow along while I tell you about them.

First of all, there's Brer Rabbit. He's a mighty fine, young lad, and he truly wishes to have Miss Molly for his girl friend.

On the other hand, there's Brer Fox who's also interested in having Miss Molly for his girl friend. But Brer Fox is somewhat sneaky when it comes to doing things in a proper way.

Miss Molly is a fine young lady, and I do believe she'd rather be Brer Rabbit's girl friend than Brer Fox's. But those two young lads haven't given her much of a chance to decide betwixt them!

Also living in the briar patch is Brer Bear . . . and Miss Honeybear, who is somewhat large around the middle . . . and Miz Skonk, who grows the best hogberries you've ever tasted . . . and Brer Terrapin, who walks like a turtle and just as slow . . . and Skonk Child, who is Miz Skonk's young'un . . . and Brer Mole and Brer Raccoon and Brer—

Well, I'll be mighty pleased if you'll read on and meet all these folks.

Boat-Builder's Battle

Now, I do believe I'll tell you about the time Brer Rabbit and Brer Fox went into the boat-building business.

'Course, they didn't work together on the boats because Brer Fox's never put himself out by helping anyone, 'specially Brer Rabbit.

It all started out one fine day when Brer Terrapin came on Brer Rabbit down by the riverbank. Brer Rabbit was piling some tree-logs together, and after watching for a time, Brer Terrapin asked, "What are you doing, Brer Rabbit?"

"I'm building a raft," Brer Rabbit explained. "I'm going to take Miss Molly for a ride on the river!"

"Miss Molly is sure to like that," Brer Terrapin said, pushing one of the raft-logs closer to the others.

"That's what I figure!" Brer Rabbit said. "And I surely appreciate your help, Brer Terrapin!"

Well, at this very time, Brer Fox was resting himself in the shade of a coolberry bush nearby, and when he heard what Brer Rabbit had said, he got an idea.

"So Brer Rabbit thinks he's going to impress Miss Molly with a boat, huh?" he said to himself. "We'll see who's impressed!"

As you know, both Brer Rabbit and Brer Fox wanted to be Miss Molly's boyfriend, but Brer Fox was always somewhat sneaky in the ways he tried to attract Miss Molly's attentions.

"I'm going to build a boat that'll truly bug Miss Molly's eyes out!" Brer Fox declared. "Then we'll see who she really likes!"

So Brer Fox took himself on down the riverbank to his house where he had plenty of wood and nails and all. Also, he figured that he wouldn't have to haul the boat very far to get it into the water. That Brer Fox is a mighty lazy feller!

Anyhow, Brer Fox went to work at chopping and sawing the boards for his boat, and Brer Raccoon came wandering past.

"I haven't seen you working so hard since the last Turnip-Pie Eating Contest!" Brer Raccoon said to Brer Fox. "Whatever is you making?"

"I'm making myself a boat!" Brer Fox bragged. "It's going to be a real luxury-type liner for sailing on the river!"

"We ain't never had a luxury-type liner floating around here!" Brer Raccoon said. "If I help you, can I ride on it a little?"

"That's fair!" Brer Fox told him, but he was really thinking that building the boat would be a lot easier if Brer Raccoon did most of the hard work. "You hunt up the wood and haul it over here, and I'll do the putting-together part!"

Well, pretty soon Brer Raccoon was piling up wood planks all around Brer Fox, and Brer Fox got the feeling that he'd seen these planks somewhere before.

"Brer Raccoon," he said at last, "where did you get these already-cut planks of wood?"

"From right over there," Brer Raccoon answered, pointing toward Brer Fox's house. "I figured you wouldn't wish to work hard at trimming down new planks when these old ones are so nearby, and they just fit!"

And when Brer Fox looked at his house, he gulped like a goldfish swallowing a honeybee!

"Brer Raccoon!" he cried out. "You've took the wall off my house!"

Sure 'nuff, Brer Raccoon had been peeling the boards from the side of Brer Fox's house and passing them over to be made into the boat!

"Brer Fox," Brer Raccoon explained, "I just made the house windows somewhat larger!"

Well, it looked to Brer Fox like all there was left of the wall was one big window!

"I'd best finish the boat-building myself," he said to Brer Raccoon. "You go find me a sail to hoist up the mast!"

"Wherever am I going to find a sail?" Brer Raccoon asked.

"That's for you to figure out," Brer Fox answered. "Just be sure it's a mighty big sail 'cause this is going to be a mighty big boat!"

So Brer Raccoon set out searching for a sail, and Brer Fox kept on hammering and nailing until he had himself a boat.

Now, that boat was somewhat out of balance and rickety-looking, but Brer Fox was sure Miss Molly would be truly impressed when he came sailing down the river in it.

Just as Brer Fox finished up his work, Brer Raccoon came hustling up with a bundle of cloth under his arm.

"Brer Fox!" he shouted. "I got the sail!"

"Toss it on board!" Brer Fox said, trying out his sailor talk. "Once we have the grand formal launching of this vessel, we'll run the sail up the mast and shiver the timbers!"

In the meantime, Brer Rabbit and Brer Terrapin had finished piecing together a fine little raft. Just as they pushed it into the river, Miss Molly came walking along.

" 'Morning, Brer Rabbit! 'Morning, Brer Terrapin!" she said most sweetly. "Whatever are you doing?"

"I built this raft so you and I could go riding on the river," Brer Rabbit told her.

"And I helped," Brer Terrapin said, somewhat shy-like.

"It's lovely!" Miss Molly said. "I do believe—"

But before she could finish saying what she was saying, Brer Raccoon came rushing up waving his arms like a windmill in a cyclone.

"Come one! Come all!" Brer Raccoon called out. "Come to the grand launching of the great ship built by Brer Fox!"

Now, right away Brer Rabbit said to himself, "Brer Fox has built himself a boat? I do believe I smell a rat that smells like Brer Fox!"

But Miss Molly was already running off to see the launching of Brer Fox's great ship!

Now, it could be that Miss Molly was playing a little trick of her own on Brer Fox. You see, he was standing right close to her, and she went ahead and smacked the jug against the boat as hard as she could.

SMASHHHH!!

The jug broke, and the molasses inside sprayed all over Brer Fox!

He truly looked foolish, but he never thought about that because he was so eager to go sailing on the river with Miss Molly!

"That was fine!" he said to Miss Molly, wiping the molasses off of his nose. "Now, let's go sailing together on the river!"

So Brer Rabbit followed along, and when they reached the riverbank in front of Brer Fox's house, all the other folks from the briar patch were gathered about.

And Brer Fox was standing on the deck of his hand-built boat in the river, grinning like a mouse filled with catnip!

"Yes, folks!" he was bragging, "this is my beautiful ship! And I'm going to ask the beautiful Miss Molly to christen it!"

Well, Miss Molly was mighty impressed by that because no one had ever asked her to christen a real live ship before!

"What an honor!" she exclaimed. "What do I do, Brer Fox?"

"See this bottle?" Brer Fox asked, holding up a little jug of molasses. "Well, you smack it against the side of the ship, and that's the christening!"

"All right!" Miss Molly agreed, and she grabbed onto that little jug. "Like this, Brer Fox?"

"Surely!" Miss Molly agreed. "That's a wonderful idea!"

Well, Brer Rabbit just stood there and felt mighty unhappy as he watched Miss Molly clamber onto Brer Fox's boat.

"Raise the anchor!" Brer Fox shouted. "Lift up the sail! This ship is about to depart for its first voyage!"

And Brer Raccoon ran up the sail he'd brought for Brer Fox . . . and Miss Honeybear let out a fearsome cry!

"That sail!" Miss Honeybear exclaimed. "It's the dress some thief stole off my clothesline today!"

Sure 'nuff, Brer Fox had told Brer Raccoon to get the biggest sail he could find, and Brer Raccoon had taken Miss Honeybear's dress for that sail!

But Miss Honeybear and Brer Rabbit were standing there on the riverbank while Brer Fox was sailing off with Miss Molly—as well as with Miss Honeybear's dress!

"Miss Honeybear," Brer Rabbit said, "I think Brer Fox is stealing Miss Molly as well as stealing your dress! And I do believe we should do something about that!"

"Sure!" Miss Honeybear said fast-like, and then she thought a bit. "But what?"

"We'll float out there on the river on the raft Brer Terrapin and I built!" Brer Rabbit declared. "And we'll beat Brer Fox at his own game!"

So Miss Honeybear and Brer Rabbit and Brer Terrapin ran to the raft.

As you know, Miss Honeybear is somewhat large, so Brer Rabbit asked her to sit in the very middle of the raft.

"And please don't jump about," he told her. "We want to float on top of the water, not in it!"

Well, Miss Honeybear sat very still so as not to tilt the raft, and Brer Rabbit and Brer Terrapin began paddling it toward Brer Fox's boat.

All this time, Brer Fox was bragging and showing off his boat to Miss Molly while Brer Raccoon kept running Miss Honeybear's dress up and down the mast, trying to make it catch the wind like a real sail.

Then all of a sudden, Brer Raccoon cried out, "Pirates! We're about to be attacked!"

Sure 'nuff, there were Brer Rabbit and Miss Honeybear and Brer Terrapin paddling their raft toward the boat!

"They aren't pirates!" Miss Molly said, laughing and waving.

"I'm not so sure about that!" Brer Fox answered. "Look at that pirate-like glare in Miss Honeybear's eyes!"

Indeed, when Miss Honeybear had caught sight of Brer Fox using her dress for a sail, she'd become somewhat angry again!

"Paddle this raft up close!" she said to Brer Rabbit. "I'm going to climb aboard that boat and rescue my dress!"

"Better get ready to jump off, Miss Molly!" Brer Rabbit warned. "Miss Honeybear is mighty large for that little boat!"

"Don't climb aboard, Miss Honeybear!" Brer Fox called out, fearful worried. "You'll sink us for sure!"

Too late! Miss Honeybear hopped on the back end of the boat, and Miss Molly jumped off the front end . . . and the back end went "ker-plunk!" right down to the bottom of the river!

"Abandon ship!" Brer Raccoon yelled and followed Miss Molly.

Yup, there was Brer Fox's ship standing straight up in the air with Brer Fox hanging onto the mast to keep from slipping into the water!

"You come down from there, Brer Fox!" Miss Honeybear said to him, giggling because

she knew the water was only up to her knees in that part of the river. "And you bring my dress with you!"

"I'm not coming down!" Brer Fox declared, and then he gulped hard. "But I do believe I'm slipping down!"

Sure 'nuff, Brer Fox couldn't hang onto the mast much longer, and there was Miss Honeybear waiting below to catch him!

"Brer Fox," she laughed, "if you let go, you'll slip right into my ever-loving arms!"

And that's just what happened!

Brer Fox slipped down, and Miss Honeybear caught him . . . and gave him a big bear hug!

"Awkkk!" Brer Fox groaned. "Stop squeezing me so hard, Miss Honeybear!"

"Tee hee!" Miss Honeybear giggled, still hugging Brer Fox. "I do believe I finally caught myself a boyfriend!"

Well, Brer Fox decided that being Miss Honeybear's boyfriend was better than getting dropped into the river—but not much better.

And Miss Molly and Brer Rabbit went floating off down the river on Brer Rabbit's raft, happy as two Junebugs in a hogberry patch!

A 'Lasses Barrel of Trouble

One fine day, Brer Fox came running through the briar patch and crying out, "Help! Thieves! Someone's stole the 'lasses barrel!"

Now, the 'lasses barrel is a wooden tub in which the folks in the briar patch make molasses, and making molasses is mighty important to them, even if it doesn't seem important to you.

So Brer Fox kept on yelling, "Help! Thieves! Help!" until he met up with Brer Rabbit.

Brer Rabbit was sitting under the honey-cone tree and whittling on a stick with his pocketknife, and when Brer Fox came racing up yelling "Help! Thieves!", Brer Rabbit kept right on whittling.

"Brer Fox," Brer Rabbit said, "I do believe you've yelled, 'Help! Thieves!' a number of times before."

Brer Rabbit was right about that, and Brer Fox tried to explain.

"The 'lasses barrel has been stole!" Brer Fox said. "It's gone! Gone! Stole for certain!"

"Maybe Skonk Child has taken it again," Brer Rabbit answered, and he went on whittling away at that piece of honeycone stick. "Maybe Skonk Child is using it for a boat and is floating around in the lake at the bottom of the briar patch!"

"Skonk Child never would steal the 'lasses barrel so clever-like!" Brer Fox declared. "This must be the work of a master criminal!"

Well, Brer Rabbit knew that once Brer Fox got a foolish idea into his head, there was no use in trying to get his head unfoolished. So Brer Rabbit felt he might as well go right on whittling and let Brer Fox do whatever he was sure to do.

"Brer Fox," he warned, "You'd best be careful about whatever you're thinking of doing."

"I'm thinking that I should trap the master criminal who's stole the 'lasses barrel!" Brer Fox answered as he stomped away. "After all, I'm the only one around here who has thief-catching equipment!"

You see, Brer Fox had once sent away to the mail-order store in Swamp Junction for a detective kit. In the kit was a fake beard and a magnifying glass; and Brer Fox was sure he could catch the thief with that equipment!

So Brer Fox tromped to his house and seized up the magnifying glass and the false beard.

"I'm ready to spy out that thief!" he said to himself. "First of all, I'll use this spying-on glass!" And he peered through the glass. "There's some feetprints on the ground right outside of my house door!"

Well, you must know that everyone who walks on his feet leaves footprints behind him, and that's what Brer Fox had done when he walked up to his house!

But he took off with his spying-on glass and followed his own footprints backward!

Now, I do believe he might've followed those prints all over the briar patch if it hadn't been for Miz Skonk and Skonk Child!

"'Morning, Brer Fox," said Miz Skonk as she saw him coming down the path toward her house.

"'Morning," Skonk Child also said. "Whatcha doing, Brer Fox?"

"Don't bother me!" Brer Fox answered, angry-like. "Can't you see that I'm peering through my spying-on glass and following these feetprints?"

"My goodness!" Miz Skonk answered. "The feetprints you're following, Brer Fox! They're your own feetprints!"

"How can they be my own feetprints?" Brer Fox asked, pointing at the marks in the dirt. "The prints is over there, and my feets is right here with the rest of me!"

"That's 'cause you've been walking around in circles!" Miz Skonk declared.

With that, Miz Skonk and Skonk Child surely did laugh, and Brer Fox scratched his jaw and thought about what they'd told him. Then he peered down through his spying-on glass at those footprints again.

"I do believe they look like my own feetprints," he said to himself. "But only in size and shape . . . and that doesn't prove anything!"

So Brer Fox put on his false beard and went on trying to track down the thief who had stolen the molasses barrel. He was sure that no one would recognize him in his disguise, but he was fearful wrong!

You see, when Brer Fox came strolling along down the road past Miss Honeybear's house, his nose smelled out a mighty fine smell!

"Hogberry pie!" he exclaimed. "I do believe I smell a true, fresh-baked hogberry pie cooling itself in Miss Honeybear's window! And I do believe it's cooled enough for me to eat it!"

Indeed, if there's one thing Brer Fox liked more than a barrel of molasses, it was a fresh-baked hogberry pie!

So he sneaked up to the window of Miss Honeybear's house and grabbed for the pie.

And Miss Honeybear came jumping right through that window to grab for him!

"Brer Fox!" she hollered. "You put that hogberry pie right back where it was cooling itself!"

"Brer who?" Brer Fox said, tugging on his false beard. "What makes you think I'm Brer Fox behind these disguising whiskers?"

"Because you're trying to steal my hogberry pie!" Miss Honeybear said right back to him.

"There's only one hogberry thief in the briar patch, and his name is Brer Fox!"

Well, Miss Honeybear was somewhat larger than Brer Fox, and he felt it was wiser to leave her hogberry pie right there where it was! As a matter of fact, he ran off down the road from Miss Honeybear's house just as fast as his feet would carry him!

But by the time he'd gotten back to his own house, he'd decided on a new plan to catch the thief who'd stolen the 'lasses barrel.

"My spying-on glass didn't work," he said to himself. "And my disguising whiskers didn't fool anyone! So I'd best turn myself into a secret agent and catch the thief that way!"

So he dressed himself up in another disguise he'd bought from the mail-order store in Swamp Junction. It was a raincoat and a pair of sunglasses, just like secret agents wear in detective books.

Brer Fox was sure that no one would recognize him in that disguise, but when he came out of his house, Miss Molly and Miss Honeybear just happened to be strolling past.

"'Morning, Brer Fox," Miss Molly said.

"Whatever are you doing in that raincoat?" Miss Honeybear asked. "It hasn't rained here in the briar patch since last Juvember, Brer Fox!"

"Don't call me Brer Fox!" Brer Fox warned them. "Can't you see that I'm disguised like one of those private eyes in the detective books?"

"A private eye?" Miss Honeybear giggled. "Brer Fox, from the way you smelled out that hogberry pie cooling in my window, I'd say you're a public nose!"

Brer Fox pretended that he hadn't heard what Miss Honeybear had said, and he put on his best smile for Miss Molly.

"Miss Molly," he said, "The detective always gets the pretty girl in the books I've read. How about going to the dance with me tonight?"

"I'm already going to the dance with Brer Rabbit," Miss Molly answered. "But I'm sure Miss Honeybear would be glad to go with you!"

Brer Fox wasn't much interested in going anywhere with Miss Honeybear, but he didn't wish to tell her that.

"Well, Miss Honeybear," he said, "I'd like to take you to the dance, but I'm very busy tracking down the thief who's stole the 'lasses barrel!"

"Tee hee!" Miss Honeybear giggled. "I'll tell you what I know about the barrel if you'll take me to the dance!"

Brer Fox really had to think about that!

He knew he'd be a hero if he tracked down the missing molasses barrel, but he truly didn't wish to dance with Miss Honeybear!

"All right," he said to Miss Honeybear at last. "Will you go to the dance with me?"

"Sure, I'll go to the dance with you!" Miss Honeybear cried out. "And—tee hee!—I don't know a thing about that barrel!"

Brer Fox blinked and gulped as Miss Molly and Miss Honeybear went away laughing.

"I don't understand it!" he said to himself. "In the books, the detective always ends up with the pretty girl . . . but it looks like I'm going to end up with Miss Honeybear tonight!"

But Brer Fox was still determined to find the molasses barrel. He was mighty certain that all the folks in the briar patch would think he was a real, honest-to-goodness hero-type if he brought back the barrel and the thieves who'd stolen it away!

So Brer Fox went searching for the barrel.

He searched high and low and all parts in-betwixt . . . but he couldn't find a trace of that molasses barrel!

Finally he came on Brer Bear and Brer Raccoon who were resting themselves under the big chickapin tree at the far end of the briar patch.

"Brer Fox," Brer Bear asked, "Why are you wearing that raincoat on such a pleasing-fine day?"

"I'm detectering!" Brer Fox answered back.

"I'm searching for the foreign-type agents who have stole the 'lasses barrel!"

"The 'lasses barrel?" Brer Raccoon wondered. "Why, the 'lasses barrel is—"

But before Brer Raccoon could finish spilling out his words, Brer Bear clumped a hand over his mouth to hush him!

"What for do you want that barrel?" Brer Bear asked Brer Fox.

"I'm going to bring it back to where it belongs!" Brer Fox answered. "That's what a detective is for!"

"You aim to bring it back?" Brer Bear asked, innocent as a hop toad in a hailstorm.

"Well, I do believe I saw it down by the riverbank, Brer Fox!"

"The riverbank!" Brer Fox shouted, and he dashed off. "That's the first real clue I've had for solving this terrible crime!"

So, as soon as Brer Fox was out of hearing, Brer Raccoon asked, "How come you told Brer Fox that, Brer Bear?"

"Watch and see!" Brer Bear answered with a most happy laugh. "Brer Fox's never helped anybody 'cept hisself, but I do believe he's about to help you and me with that 'lasses barrel!"

Sure 'nuff, Brer Fox tromped his big feet right down to the riverbank. And sure 'nuff, there was the molasses barrel setting right by the waterside!

"I done it!" cried Brer Fox. "I detectived out the 'lasses barrel and saved it from the spy-type folk who stole it!"

220

"You and Brer Raccoon?" Brer Fox asked, his eyes bugging out. "You two was the fearsome foreign agents who stole the 'lasses barrel?"

"We never stole it!" Brer Raccoon objected, somewhat angry-like.

"We took it down to the river to fill it with lemonade-making water for the dance tonight," Brer Bear explained to Brer Fox. "But when it was filled up, it was too heavy for us to haul back!"

That's right: Brer Fox had helped out the folks without knowing he was helping!

If he'd known, I do believe he never would've done it because that's the kind of feller he is!

On the other hand, Brer Fox had promised to take Miss Honeybear to the dance, and maybe that was the reward he deserved! You see, his muscles were somewhat sore from hauling the barrel filled with water for the lemonade, but after getting danced around by Miss Honeybear, he couldn't feel a thing!

Yup, like Brer Rabbit said to Miss Molly while they were dancing, "Sometimes Brer Fox does nice things . . . 'specially if he doesn't know he's doing them!"

Now, the molasses barrel was always kept at the town hall where all the folks could make use of it when they wished to.

So Brer Fox wished to haul it back to where it belonged, only he didn't count on its being so fearful heavy!

"This barrel must be full up to the brim with 'lasses!" he said to himself as he lifted it up and started hauling it away. "I do believe the folks'll give me a fine reward for bringing it back!"

Wherefore, Brer Fox huffed and puffed and dragged the barrel all the way to the town hall.

Well, as soon as he'd plunked that barrel right down where it belonged, Brer Bear and Brer Raccoon popped themselves out from where they'd been hiding and watching.

"Thank you, Brer Fox," Brer Bear said, most happy-like. "That surely was helpful of you to bring the barrel up from the riverside where Brer Raccoon and I left it!"

ANNUAL CROSS SWAMP ROAD RACE

TOWN HALL

Rabbit Racer Versus Fox Flyer

Every year about this time, the folks in the briar patch hold the Great Annual Road Race, and I do believe I should tell you about that race.

First of all, there's only one road in the briar patch, which is the same road everyone uses every day. If you start off on that road, you circle clear around the briar patch and when you finish up, you're right back where you started out!

Also, no one really plans ahead for the race. One day, Judge Owl puts up a sign announcing the Great Annual Road Race, and that turns out to be the day it's held. Of course, Judge Owl starts the race and declares the winner when it's over, and that's why the folks call him "Judge."

It's also important for you to know that Miss Molly awards the Trophy Cup to the winner, and that's why Brer Fox and Brer

Rabbit always enter the race. Those two fellers are mighty fond of Miss Molly, and whoever gets the Trophy Cup also gets to take Miss Molly to the Victory Dinner and Fireworks Display which is held afterward.

As a matter of fact, Brer Rabbit and Brer Fox are usually the only fellers who bother racing before the dining and fireworks-watching.

Now that you know all that, I'll get on with telling you about last year's race.

One day, Brer Rabbit came walking down the road, and there was Brer Raccoon standing by the honeycone tree outside of the town hall.

"Look, Brer Rabbit!" Brer Raccoon called. "Judge Owl's put up the sign declaring the Great Annual Road Race!"

Sure 'nuff, there was the Judge's sign nailed up on the tree!

"It seems somewhat early in the year for the race," Brer Rabbit said, thoughtful-like.

"It's never too early for eating the Victory Dinner and watching the fireworks!" Brer Raccoon replied. "Do you think you can win the race again this year, Brer Rabbit?"

"Sure!" Brer Rabbit exclaimed. "Brer Fox'll never beat me as long as I'm driving the 'Rabbit Racer'!"

Now, the Rabbit Racer was a mighty swift vehicle which Brer Rabbit had built himself by hooking some old wheelbarrow wheels on a big wooden box he'd found out in back of Brer Bear's store. It didn't have a gasoline motor or any of those city-type things, but it'd always rolled fast enough to beat Brer Fox.

"We'd best get the Racer fixed up proper-like," Brer Raccoon suggested. "The last I seen, Skonk Child was playing with it down by the riverbank just before the big rain storm!"

So Brer Rabbit and Brer Raccoon set off to find the Rabbit Racer. What they didn't know was that Brer Fox had been hiding himself behind the honeycone tree and listening to everything they'd said!

"Ho, ho, ho!" Brer Fox laughed to himself. "I've got a surprise for Brer Rabbit! I'm going to win the race this year, and Miss Molly along with the Trophy Cup!"

As you know, Brer Fox can be mighty sneaky when he wishes to be, but I'm not going to tell you what he planned just yet.

Now, when Brer Rabbit and Brer Raccoon found the Racer down by the river, it was in fearsome shape. It was buried up to the wheel-rims in mud from the rain storm, and it was plain falling apart!

Well, they hauled it up on the bankside and scraped off all that mud, and then Brer Raccoon gave it a fresh coat of lemon-flower paint while Brer Rabbit smeared lightning-bug grease on the wheels to make it go faster.

When they were finally done, they both agreed that the Racer looked as good as new, which wasn't saying much because it hadn't looked very special when it'd been truly new!

After that, Brer Rabbit and Brer Raccoon pushed the Racer all the way to the starting line for the race. All the folks were gathered

there in front of the town hall, including Miss Molly and Miss Honeybear.

"Brer Rabbit," Miss Molly said, "I surely hope you win so we can go to the Victory Dinner together!"

"I don't care who wins!" Miss Honeybear declared. "Just as long as there's plenty to eat at that dinner!" And then she looked down the road and blinked with surprise. "Goodness! Here comes Brer Fox, and just look at his race-type car!"

Remember that surprise Brer Fox had said he'd have for Brer Rabbit? Well, that sneaky Brer Fox had sent off to the mail-order store in Swamp Junction and bought himself the newest and fastest and flashiest racer in the catalog!

"Good day, ladies!" Brer Fox called, smiling like a bullfrog eating sassafras. "Good day, Brer Rabbit! I understand there's to be a racing-type competition today, and I expects to win with my fine new 'Fox Flyer'!"

Before Brer Rabbit could answer, Judge Owl hauled himself out in front of the folks.

"Time for the race!" he declared. "Let's get it over with so we can start eating the Victory Dinner!"

"I agrees!" Miss Honeybear said. "All this waiting around is making me hungry!"

"Everything makes you hungry, Miss Honeybear!" Judge Owl grumbled.

Well, while everyone else was listening to Judge Owl and Miss Honeybear, Brer Fox set out to play a trick on Brer Rabbit! He'd brought along a big rope, and when no one was watching, he tied one end of it to the back of the Rabbit Racer and the other end to the honeycone tree!

"Brer Rabbit," Brer Fox chuckled as he climbed into his car, "I hope you get back in time to see Miss Molly give me the Trophy Cup!"

"Brer Fox," Brer Rabbit warned, "don't count your trophies before they're won!"

Judge Owl jumped out of the way and waved his tall silk hat.

"Ready!" he shouted. "Get set . . . GO!!"

And the Great Annual Road Race began!

Only Brer Rabbit's Racer didn't move an inch!

"Hey!" he cried. "What's happening?"

"Nothing's happening, that's what's happening!" Brer Raccoon told him as Brer Fox went rolling down the road. "It seems like your Racer has got itself tied to the honey-cone tree!"

Sure 'nuff, that rope Brer Fox had tied to the back of Brer Rabbit's car was holding it still as a turkey at sundown!

"Cut me loose!" Brer Rabbit begged. "Cut me loose!"

"Hang on, Brer Rabbit!" Brer Raccoon warned as he picked up a hatchet-ax and swung it at the rope. "You is about to be launched!"

WHOMP! Brer Raccoon surely did cut the Rabbit Racer loose, and Brer Rabbit went rolling off to catch up with Brer Fox.

Now, Brer Fox had himself a good start on Brer Rabbit, but the Rabbit Racer spun along fast as could be. For one thing, Brer Rabbit and Brer Raccoon had put a mighty

lot of lightning-bug grease on the wheels which made them turn quicker than you'd think possible. Also, Brer Fox was slowed down somewhat because he'd loaded up the Fox Flyer with a number of things to use in tricking Brer Rabbit!

The first of those tricks was a sack of chicken feathers!

Indeed, Brer Rabbit was nearly caught up to Brer Fox when this great cloud of white came blowing out of the Fox Flyer.

"What's that?" Brer Rabbit asked himself. "A whirly wind? A snowy storm?"

But when Brer Rabbit drove into that cloud, he knew for sure what it was!

"Chicken feathers!" he exclaimed. "That sneaky Brer Fox is trying to slow me down with his tricks!"

But that trick of Brer Fox's didn't work very well. You see, as soon as Brer Rabbit cleared his way through that feather-cloud, he started gaining on Brer Fox again!

Oh, I do wish you could've seen the look

225

on Brer Fox's face when he peered back and saw Brer Rabbit right behind him! I do believe he was as angry as he could get, which is mighty angry!

"The feathers slowed Brer Rabbit a little, but not enough for me to win!" Brer Fox said. "It's a good thing I brung along a real slower-down for him!"

Well, Brer Fox had stashed a barrel of molasses in his Flyer, and he poured that molasses all over the road where Brer Rabbit was sure to drive into it!

I do believe that's there's nothing in this whole world that's as sticky and slippery as the molasses the folks make in the briar patch!

Sure 'nuff, when Brer Rabbit drove into that puddle of molasses, his racing car stuck something fierce!

"I'm in a sea of 'lasses!" Brer Rabbit cried out. "That sly old Brer Fox has stopped me for sure!"

But like I told you, that molasses was also terrible slippery, and before Brer Rabbit knew it, the Racer had slipped right off the road and into the middle of Miz Skonk's hogberry patch!

Now everyone knows that Miz Skonk grows the finest hogberries in the briar patch, and when she heard the crashing of the Rabbit Racer in her field, she came storming out of her house.

"Brer Rabbit!" she hollered. "What is you doing race-driving through my hogberry field?"

"It seems like I'm making a detour," Brer Rabbit said. "The road's filled up with 'lasses, Miz Skonk!"

"Goodness!" Miz Skonk said. "This is the first time I've heard of the road being filled up with 'lasses!"

"Well," Brer Rabbit explained, "this is the first time Brer Fox's been ahead of me in the Great Annual Road Race!"

Miz Skonk gazed on the Racer setting in the middle of her field, and she thought for a moment.

"Brer Rabbit," she said at last, "it looks like you is already halfway through my hog-

berry patch, so you might as well drive on through the other half! You'll come out on the road again, and maybe you can still catch up with Brer Fox!"

"Thanks, Miz Skonk!" Brer Rabbit called as he rolled the Racer on through the field. "That's most kindly of you!"

Miz Skonk watched Brer Rabbit's car cross her hogberry patch, and she chuckled to herself.

"My!" she said, happy-like. "I do believe Brer Rabbit's squashed up enough berries for a year's supply of hogberry jam!"

Sure 'nuff, when Brer Rabbit finished his detour through Miz Skonk's field, he was right back on the road and close behind Brer Fox once more!

When Brer Fox saw that his tricks hadn't worked, he was super-angry, mostly because he'd run out of more tricks to play on Brer Rabbit!

So the two cars came rolling down the road close as could be, but Brer Fox was still just a mite-bit ahead!

Now, I should tell you about the place where the road around the briar patch splits itself in two directions. One direction goes down to the swamp and back to the starting place, and the other goes out over Jump-Off Point and straight down to the town hall.

Well, Brer Fox was so feared of losing the race to Brer Rabbit that he ran his Flyer off onto the shortcut to Jump-Off Point!

On the other hand, when Brer Rabbit reached that dividing point in the road, he did what was smarter and took the swamp turn. He knew well enough that going over Jump-Off Point was just plain foolish!

But Brer Fox sped to Jump-Off Point . . . and out to the edge . . . and over . . . and downhill . . . and it wasn't until he saw a road sign that said "Danger! Apply Brakes!" that he realized just how foolish he'd been!

Brer Fox had bought the finest race-type car from the mail-order store in Swamp Junction, but it didn't have any brakes to slow it down!

And there he was, zipping down the hill from Jump-Off Point toward the finish line of the Great Annual Road Race, but there was no way he could stop the Fox Flyer!

Also, Miss Molly and Brer Bear and Brer Raccoon and Judge Owl and Miss Honeybear were all standing in the road, waiting for the winner of the race to cross the finish line . . . and Miss Honeybear was right in the middle of the road!

"Get out of the way, Miss Honeybear!" Brer Fox warned. "Not even you can stop me!"

KEEERRRROOOOOMMMMMM!!

Yup, Brer Fox ran right into Miss Honeybear, and she landed on the front of his car, laughing and smiling through the windshield at Brer Fox!

"Hi, Brer Fox," she said, between her giggles. "Where're we going?"

"I don't know!" Brer Fox answered, mighty excited-like. "I can't see where we're going 'cause you're blocking the view with your somewhat-large self!"

But Brer Fox had been right about one thing. Not even Miss Honeybear could stop the Fox Flyer! In fact, the weight she added made it go even faster, and they shot off down the road as if the race was starting all over again!

Well, they were almost out of sight when Brer Rabbit rolled up looking sad as a grasshopper in winter.

228

"I guess I lost the race," he said to Judge Owl and the others. "Brer Fox won, huh?"

"Not exactly," Judge Owl declared wisely. "The Trophy Cup goes to the driver who finishes first! But as far as we knows, Brer Fox still hasn't finished!"

So Miss Molly gave Brer Rabbit the Trophy Cup, and they went to the Victory Dinner and Fireworks Display together.

And for all I know, Brer Fox and Miss Honeybear are still zipping around and around the briar patch in the Fox Flyer!

Peter Pan and
The Friendly Crocodile

It all began the day the crocodile got sick. As everyone knows, the crocodile who lives in Never Land once ate Captain Hook's hand. He liked it so much that from that time on he followed Hook everywhere, hoping to get the rest of him. Luckily for the pirate, the crocodile had also swallowed a clock. The clock continued to tick merrily away inside the croc, and the ticking warned Hook when the crocodile was near. Hook soon became expert at making quick departures whenever he heard the tell-tale ticking.

One day, when the crocodile was practicing his backstroke in the lagoon, he met the lost boys. They were having a picnic on the beach. The lost boys rather liked the crocodile. Any enemy of Captain Hook was a friend of theirs. So they offered the croc some bran muffins, which they had baked themselves. Sad to say, they had misread the recipe and put in too much mustard. The poor crocodile immediately got indigestion.

The lost boys were very upset, so they led the groaning croc to their home and dosed him well with bicarbonate of soda.

That morning Captain Hook awoke in fine fettle. "It's a beautiful day," said he, when Mr. Smee brought his breakfast. "I think I'll go out and stir up some trouble!"

"Watch out for the crocodile," warned Mr. Smee.

"Aye," said Hook. "That beast is always on my trail. If he hadn't swallowed that clock, he'd have gotten me long ago. That blasted tick-tocking has saved me many a time."

Then Hook firmly put all thoughts of the crocodile out of his mind. He ordered Mr. Smee to lower the dinghy and row him to Skull Rock. When he got there he listened carefully for the ticking of the clock. All was silent. The crocodile wasn't about. So Hook carved his initials on Skull Rock. It was something he'd always wanted to do.

On went the pirate to Mermaid Lagoon. Hook couldn't hear the crocodile ticking there, so he stole all of the mermaids' coral combs.

Hook then told Mr. Smee to row to the Indian camp. When he arrived there he did not hear the tick-tock of the croc, so he stole two Indian totem poles and a teepee and made off with them, chuckling an evil chuckle.

"That awful crocodile must have left Never Land!" chortled Hook. "I don't have a care in the world! Oh, what nasty thing shall I do to celebrate?"

"Why not kidnap the lost boys?" suggested Mr. Smee, who liked to be helpful.

"Just the thing!" cried Hook. "Mr. Smee, let us plot!"

While Hook was plotting, the Indian Chief came to the tree house where Peter Pan and the lost boys lived. "Wicked pirate steal totems," complained the Chief. "Where is crocodile who keeps wicked pirate in line?"

Peter had to admit that the crocodile was right there in the tree house. What's more, the croc was still too sick to thwart Hook's evil plans. Peter and the lost boys held a conference.

"Since the croc can't stop Hook, we'll have to find some other way," said Peter.

"What way?" wondered Foxy. "We don't have long sharp teeth like croc. Hook isn't afraid of us!"

"Wait," said Peter. "We don't really need the croc to scare Hook. All we need are a lot of loud clocks. If Hook hears anything tick, he'll run so fast he'll never look to see whether the crocodile is behind him or not."

"But we don't have any clocks," Cubby pointed out.

"There are lots of clocks in London," said Peter Pan. "We can borrow some from Wendy."

So Peter Pan flew off to London and talked to Wendy Darling. She was very helpful. She borrowed an alarm clock from her mother. She gave Peter the clock that stood on the shelf in the nursery. When the cook wasn't looking, she took the kitchen clock. She even borrowed a clock from Nana, the nursemaid dog. Soon Peter had his arms full of clocks, all ticking loudly. Well satisfied, Peter flew back to Never Land.

He was just in time, for night was falling and Captain Hook had sailed his ship right up Crocodile Creek. He planned to land and march his pirate crew straight to the lost boys' tree home. Peter quickly put a clock in the tall grass on the bank of the creek. When Hook stepped ashore he heard the ominous "Tick-tock!" He turned and rushed back to the safety of his ship.

"Hah!" said Hook to himself. "Now I know that the crocodile is in Crocodile Creek, I'll land at the Indian camp."

But as Hook came within sight of the Indian village he heard a "Tick-tock!" from the clock which Peter Pan had hidden under the bluffs. Hook turned five shades of green and ordered a quick retreat.

The pirate ship sailed toward Skull Rock. But Peter had hidden Mrs. Darling's alarm clock in one of the hollows of the rock. When Hook approached, the clock not only ticked—the alarm went off with a clanging jangle!

Hook's hair stood on end. He clutched at Mr. Smee in terror. "Save me, Smee!" he pleaded. "That crocodile is everywhere!"

Smee ordered the ship back to Pirate Cove, and there Captain Hook took to his bed with a bad case of nerves. By the time Hook was able to sail abroad again, the crocodile was feeling well and healthy and was looking for Hook with renewed relish.

As for the clocks, Peter Pan flew to London with them, arriving just before dawn. Wendy put every clock back where it belonged, and Mrs. Darling's alarm clock rang in time to awaken the Darling family for breakfast. So no one was wiser. Except Wendy, of course.

Donald Duck and The Witch

It was getting on toward Halloween.

Donald Duck and his nephews were hunting for pumpkins for Jack-o-lanterns.

The day was almost over, and red and gold clouds were piling up in the sky, when they found a field that was full of pumpkins perfect for them.

They were walking back to the farm house, each with a round, ripe pumpkin in his arms, when Huey stopped them all with a shout.

236

"Look! A witch on a broomstick!" he cried.

They all saw a dark form streak across the sky.

"Pooh!" said Donald. "Witches, pooh! There are no witches, you know that. It must have been some sort of a bird you saw."

But the boys were not convinced.

Next day they set out to look for the witch. They had a long, hard walk through the tangled woods. There was no path to follow, and they were not even sure just what they hoped to find.

At last they heard a cackling laugh up ahead. And what could be a surer sign of a witch than a crickling, cackling laugh?

"Sh!" said Dewey, with his fingers on his lips. And he led the way through the underbrush into the clearing beyond.

There stood a crooked little house, clearly the home of a witch. From the crooked little chimney rose a thread of smoke.

Smoke and steam rolled up in clouds from a cauldron out in front. And through the smoke came that merry, scary sound, the cackling laugh of a witch.

"Welcome, boys, welcome," said the witch's voice. "Welcome to Witch Hazel's little home." Then she came hobbling toward them,

a merry little sprite, grinning with witchery glee.

The boys were speechless with surprise.

"What can I do for you today?" Witch Hazel asked of them. "Any spells you'd like me to cast? Anybody you'd like to bewitch?" And her elbow poked Louie in the ribs, while she gave him a sly wink.

"Bewitch!" echoed Louie.

"Cast spells!" said Dewey.

"Unca Donald!" cried Huey.

They all agreed. They told Witch Hazel how Donald refused to believe in her or any other witch.

"We'll show him!" she cackled, beckoning them close.

From the pockets of her dress she tossed bits of this and that into her steaming pot.

"A real witch's brew!" gasped Dewey Duck, as swirls of smoke in mysterious shapes began to rise and blow.

"We'll show that Donald!" Witch Hazel vowed. "You meet me here on Halloween."

Home went the boys and they said not a word about their adventure to Donald Duck.

Donald was not surprised when the boys disappeared early on Halloween.

He was not surprised when his doorbell rang soon after dark that night. There beneath the porch light stood the boys. Donald chuckled as he recognized them through their disguises. They were dressed as witches, one and all.

"Come in," said Donald with a grin, holding his door open wide. They parked their broomsticks beside the door. Donald rubbed

his eyes as he thought he saw one jump. That, he knew, could not have been.

In came the witches, one, two, three. No, there were one, two, three, four!

Donald was surprised, but he did not say a word as they all took seats around the room.

"Treats?" he asked, passing a tray of fancy little cakes.

"Ouch!" cried Dewey, who reached for

one first. A mouse trap was stuck on his thumb.

"Wow!" cried Louie, who reached for one next. It turned out to be a jack-in-the-box.

"Glub!" gulped Huey, when he bit into his. It was all made of rubber, you see.

"Thanks," said the fourth guest with a cackling laugh. She blew at her cake, and it exploded into dust, right in Donald's face.

"Serves you right, smartie," said a voice. Donald whirled around. There were only the Jack-o-lanterns sitting there, grinning saucily. But as Donald looked, it seemed to him that the merry faces shook with glee.

"We must be leaving now," one witch said. "Won't you come with us, and let us return your hospitality?"

"No, thanks," said Donald, clinging to the

doorknob as they all swept him out onto the porch.

It was four against one. He soon found himself astride a broomstick.

"Abracadabra, boys! Here we go!" he heard a voice cackle in his ear.

All around him he saw broomsticks *fly*—and to his horror Donald saw the ground sink away below him, too!

Over the treetops and straight toward the moon the broomstick pointed—then down to the woods.

"Welcome to Witch Hazel's little home," he heard the cackling voice say. And down tumbled Donald—down, down, down into the witch's pot!

"Ho, ho, ho!" laughed the other three. He knew his nephews' voices all too well.

Donald gasped and sputtered. And he sizzled with rage when they hauled him out, soaking wet to the skin.

The witches did not notice. They were all doubled over, laughing.

Witch Hazel disappeared into her little

house, and came back with an extra dress and hat.

"Better put on something dry," she told Donald with a grin. And he stamped off into the house.

When he came out again, a table was set close beside the bubbling pot. Three Jack-o-lanterns glowed on a Halloween feast—pumpkin pie and apple tart and corn on the cob and all sorts of delicious things.

244

"Have a real treat, Unca Donald," the nephews said, coming out from behind their masks.

So they all sat down and ate their fill—yes, Witch Hazel, too.

After a while, even Donald could smile.

"I still don't believe in witches," he said to Witch Hazel with a courtly bow. "But if there were any, I'd want them all to be just exactly like you."

245

Donald Duck
and
The Light-Fingered Genie

As we all know, Donald Duck makes his home in Duckburg, a town which is noted for many things. There is the Duckburg First National Bank and the Duckburg Second National Bank, and these belong to Uncle Scrooge McDuck. There is the Duckburg Water Works and the Duckburg Power Plant, and these also belong to Uncle Scrooge. There is the McDuck Memorial Statue in the town square, the Duckburg Library, and the McDuck Zoo. And there is, of course, the McDuck Money Bin, the world's largest vault for the storage of ten dollar bills, five dollar bills, one dollar bills, quarters, dimes, nickels, pennies, and—above all—gold! Uncle Scrooge dearly loves gold.

On the morning our story commences, Uncle Scrooge was pleased enough with his banks and his water works and his power plant, and even his statue in the town square.

He wasn't at all pleased with his money bin. His money bin, on that sad morning, contained only thirty-two thousand cubic yards of gold—give or take a bushel or two —and Uncle Scrooge wasn't feeling like the richest duck in the world. He was feeling like a poor old duck, and an angry duck. And when Uncle Scrooge was angry, Donald usually knew it before anyone else.

"Uncle Scrooge, please don't carry on so," Donald begged. "You *are* still the world's richest duck and . . . "

"And I won't be for long if this keeps up," snapped Scrooge. "Now get out of here. Go on. I don't want to see you again till you come up with an idea—a good idea."

Poor Donald. There was nothing to do but to go trailing home to the little cottage he shared with his three nephews.

"What's the matter now, Unca Donald?" asked Huey.

"Did Unca Scrooge fire you again?" Louie wanted to know.

"That makes the third time this week," said Dewey.

"I know! I know!" Donald crept into the house and slumped down in his shabby old armchair.

"Uncle Scrooge wants me to find a way

to stop J. P. Thimblerig," he told the boys.

"Thimblerig the zillionaire?" asked Dewey.

"Who else?" said Donald. "Old Thimblerig is almost as rich as Uncle Scrooge, and he's getting richer every day. If Uncle Scrooge flies to the Andes to inspect a diamond mine, Thimblerig is there ahead of him. If there really are any diamonds in the mine, Thimblerig has bought it before Uncle Scrooge's plane ever lands. Last week there was a gold strike in Matagona, and Thimblerig leased the whole country. I've thought and thought, but there just isn't any way to stop the old codger."

"There's got to be a way," said Dewey.

"You're tired," said Louie. "What you need is a day off."

"Why don't we take our scuba gear and go diving?" suggested Huey.

Donald didn't argue. He knew it wouldn't do any good to sit brooding in an armchair. So he and the boys packed their diving masks and their swim fins into Donald's little car, and they headed for Brewster's Beach.

"Old pirate ships used to anchor in the bay off the beach," said Louie. "Maybe you'll find some sunken treasure, so you won't have to worry about a job with Uncle Scrooge."

"Fat chance," said Donald, but he was really ready to try anything—anything at all.

So for hours he swam and searched and paddled and dove and, as the sun began to go down, he did find something washed up on a sandbar. He found a jug.

"Some treasure!" snorted Donald, and he was about to throw it back into the water when a man came striding along the beach —a man with a kindly face and bright sparkling eyes.

"Why, you found the jug!" said the man.

"What about it?" Donald asked.

"If you'll take a word of advice," said the man, "you'll throw it back into the bay."

antique. It wasn't a collector's item, either. It was only a jug which had been made for the Good and Sticky Molasses Company. "And they've only been in business for five years," moaned Donald.

He was about to toss it into the trash can when the jug suddenly said, "Careful there!"

Now a talking jug may not be an antique, but it certainly is not like an ordinary, everyday molasses container. Donald began to shake, and he shook so hard that he almost dropped the jug on the floor.

"Don't do that!" snapped the voice from the jug. "You're jiggling my turban!"

"Your turban?" echoed Donald.

"Certainly. All genies wear turbans," said the voice from the jug. "Don't you know anything."

"A genie!" cried one of the boys.

"Of course it's a genie!" said another. "Only genies live in jugs and bottles and lamps."

And the man turned away and walked on.

Donald and the boys looked at one another, and they looked after the man and they stared at the jug. And a very suspicious idea came into Donald's head. "If I throw the jug back," he said to his nephews, "that man can come and get it. Boys, I have a feeling this jug is valuable."

"Maybe it's a rare antique," said Louie.

"Maybe it's a collector's item!" cried Dewey.

"Lots of people collect old bottles and jugs," added Huey.

But when Donald and the boys got the jug home, they discovered it wasn't a rare

Donald put the jug down very, very carefully. "Are you really a genie?" he asked.

"Naturally, I am," said the voice. "The boy's right. Only genies live in jugs, and I must say I'm very tired of this one."

"Open it up, Unca Donald!" cried Huey. "Let him out."

"Genies can get you anything you want," said Dewey. "They can get you palaces and emeralds and rubies and gold."

"You did find a treasure, Unca Donald," put in Louie. "Now you'll never have to worry about your job with Unca Scrooge again."

"Wait a minute!" said Donald. "Remember the story of the fisherman who let the genie out of the bottle? The genie was so angry after being in the jug, he almost killed the poor fisherman."

"That genie had been shut up too long," said the voice from the jug. "I've only been here for a couple of hours. Let me out and I'll give you anything your heart desires. And don't stand there talking about it all week. This silly jug reeks of molasses."

So Donald, who was truly good-hearted, pulled the cork out of the jug.

Pouff! A cloud of smoke wafted out and filled the kitchen. Then, very quickly, the smoke became a genie—a skinny, somewhat cranky-looking genie who dripped molasses on the kitchen floor.

"My name is Abdul," said the genie, "and I believe the first thing I need is a bath."

No one could deny this. Anyone, even a genie, who has been inside a molasses jug needs a bath. So Abdul the genie hurried up to the bathroom and had a nice scrub, and if he used up all the hot water, who could complain? He *had* been terribly sticky.

When he finished his bath, he wrapped himself cozily in Donald's bathrobe and announced that he simply had to have some new clothes.

"New clothes?" echoed Donald. "But can't you fly to genie land, or wherever it is that genies go, and get some there?"

"In these?" Abdul held up the clothes he had been wearing when he came out of the jug. "I can't go home looking like a candy factory. These are full of molasses. One has one's pride, you know."

Donald sighed and took out his wallet. "Okay," he said to the boys. "Take this and run down to the shopping center and get Abdul something to wear."

"Something with stripes," said the genie. "I'm very partial to stripes."

The three young ducks took Donald's wallet and they ran down to the shopping center, where they bought a nice striped jacket and a handsome pair of slacks and a new shirt and shoes and socks and everything a genie needs to make him look like a credit to his profession.

While they were gone, Donald took his own bath. The water was cold, but one must put up with a few inconveniences when one has a genie in the house.

The genie put on his new clothes and looked at himself in the mirror and decided that he was an extraordinarily handsome genie.

"And I'm starved," said he. "Let's all go out to dinner."

"Out to dinner?" Donald was horrified. "Do you think I'm made of money?"

"Actually, my noble friend, you don't look as if you are," said Abdul. "But don't forget, I *am* a genie. I can get you all the money you want."

"And diamonds and rubies and sapphires and emeralds?" asked Dewey.

"Don't forget about palaces," said Huey.

"And gold and silver," added Louie.

"All in good time," said the genie. "Dinner first; treasure later. I can't do my best work on an empty stomach."

It was soon clear that Abdul could do quite a bit on an empty stomach. First of all, he did not approve of Donald's humble little car. "No class," he said. "No class at all." And he suddenly disappeared.

He was back a moment later with a "Pop!" And there, standing at the curb, was a dream of a car—a long, low, gleaming, elegant, expensive sports car.

"You drive," he told Donald. "I happen not to have a driver's license. I'm kept rather busy—when I'm not in a jug, you know. I never have time to take the examination."

Donald joyfully climbed behind the wheel. The three thrilled nephews happily got into the back seat. And Abdul sat in front, so that he could direct Donald to the marvelous seafood restaurant down on the shore.

"I can't wait to get there," said Abdul. "You work up quite an appetite sitting around in a molasses jug."

"It looks as if you'll have to wait," said Donald. He pointed ahead. "The drawbridge over the creek is up and traffic is stopped."

"Nonsense!" cried Abdul. "I never wait if I can help it. Be back in half a minute."

Again Abdul disappeared.

"Maybe he's going to bring a magic carpet," said Louie.

But Abdul didn't bring a magic carpet. This time, when he appeared, he brought a helicopter. "Forget the car," he advised. "I can get another one any time."

So Donald and the nephews got out of

the car and into the helicopter and clattered along to that marvelous restaurant, where Abdul landed the helicopter on the roof.

"How are we going to get down from here?" asked Donald. "Are you going to pop off and bring back a ladder?"

"You lack imagination, my friend," said Abdul, and he popped off to whatever mysterious place he knew and was back in a moment with a flying carpet.

"If you could get a flying carpet, why did we bother with a helicopter?" Donald asked, very reasonably.

"This is a secondhand carpet," explained Abdul. "It's only good for short hauls."

And he and Donald and the boys used it to zip down off the roof to the restaurant entrance, where Abdul stowed the carpet in the shrubbery "One wouldn't want to lose

even a secondhand flying carpet," said he, and they went into the restaurant.

Once they were inside, Abdul ordered a marvelous meal for everyone. And after dinner, when all the ducks were as full of good things as they could be, the waiter brought the check and Abdul added it up. He found it was quite correct. And he disappeared.

"Don't worry," Donald told the waiter. "He'll be right back. He always is."

Abdul *was* right back. He had a wad of crisp new money which he handed to Donald, and Donald paid the waiter.

So the day, which had started out on such a gloomy note, ended very happily—except for one or two little items.

When the ducks left the restaurant, a number of large men in uniform were waiting for them.

One man wanted to know how Donald had gotten hold of the new experimental helicopter which was parked on the roof.

Another man wanted to know why Donald had swiped Pilkington Playboy's Blooper V-10 sports car and then abandoned it on the road.

And the waiter soon hurried out, clutching the money Donald had given him. It was, he said, counterfeit.

The only thing that wasn't either counterfeit or stolen was the magic carpet, and Abdul hurried the three nephews onto this and flew home to Donald's little cottage on the edge of Duckburg.

Uncle Scrooge was summoned, and he came, which was a thing Uncle Scrooge always did when Donald really got into trouble. He explained things as well as he could, which wasn't very well, and he paid poor Donald's bail. Then he drove Donald home and Donald tottered into the house and dropped into his own worn armchair.

"Where did you get your sticky mitts on a wad of counterfeit bills?" Donald asked

Abdul. "I can understand about the sports car and the helicopter, but where did you get the fake money?"

"Oh, that was easy," said the genie proudly. "I made it. I've had a little printing press for some time. I thought the money looked very nice."

"Well, the treasury people didn't!" shouted Donald. "Uncle Scrooge didn't, either."

Abdul's feelings were hurt. Genies are sensitive. They don't like to be shouted at. "Careful!" he warned, "or I'll get back in my jug."

"Please do!" yelled Donald.

Abdul sniffed. "You simply don't appreciate me. I would get back in the jug—I truly would—but it's so sticky."

"Huey, go out to the kitchen and wash that jug!" ordered Donald.

Huey went. In fact, he ran. It didn't take him two minutes to get the jug sparkly clean.

"You'll be sorry," warned Abdul, and he turned himself back into a puff of smoke and vanished into the jug.

"So much for genies," said Donald, as he thunked the stopper into the jug. He and the boys then got into their own humble little car and drove to Brewster's Beach, where they planned to hurl the jug, Abdul and all, into the bay.

Who should come strolling along the beach but that kindly looking man with the bright, sparkling eyes.

"You look as if you've had a rough day," said the kindly man. "I see you didn't take my advice. You kept the jug, and you opened it."

"How did you know?" asked Donald.

"You look haunted. You look the way I did after I found a certain bottle in the surf. And I see that you're using my molasses jug to get a certain genie back where he should be. Glad it came in handy."

With that, the kindly little man walked on.

Donald stared at the molasses jug and he thought and he thought. Suppose he threw the jug back into the bay. Suppose someone else found it. Suppose someone else released Abdul the genie.

Then Donald had a perfectly brilliant idea. Someone *should* find it—someone who had been making trouble for Uncle Scrooge, and thus for Donald and the boys. So Donald hurried back home, and he made a telephone call.

At noon the next day he was in Uncle Scrooge's office in the money bin.

"I am not speaking to you," said Uncle Scrooge. "Also, I told you not to show your face here again until you came up with an idea that would stop old Thimblerig from buying up all the gold mines and diamond fields and . . . "

"Just turn on the television set, Uncle Scrooge," said Donald. "We're in time to watch the twelve o'clock news."

The twelve o'clock news was well worth watching. The newsman was reporting that Zillionaire Thimblerig was busy trying to explain how the yacht "Mitania," which did not belong to him, had been found on the lawn of his palatial estate.

"Donald, did you do that somehow?" asked Uncle Scrooge.

Donald only grinned a happy grin.

"How did you do it?" demanded Uncle Scrooge.

"I had a special messenger deliver a molasses jug to Mr. Thimblerig," said Donald, and he never explained any further.

He never explained, but you know. And if you ever find a jug floating in the bay near Brewster's Beach—especially if it's a molasses jug—send the jug to Arabia or put it on the cupboard shelf or perhaps bury it under the cellar floor. Never, never open it, because genies are not what they used to be. Perhaps they never were!